Escape from Pakistan

**The untold story of
Commodore Jack Shea**

ESCAPE FROM PAKISTAN

The untold story of
Commodore Jack Shea

DEBORA ANN SHEA

**PENGUIN
ENTERPRISE**

An imprint of Penguin Random House

PENGUIN ENTERPRISE

USA | Canada | UK | Ireland | Australia
New Zealand | India | South Africa | China

Penguin Enterprise is part of the Penguin Random House group of companies
whose addresses can be found at global.penguinrandomhouse.com

Published by Penguin Random House India Pvt. Ltd
4th Floor, Capital Tower 1, MG Road,
Gurugram 122 002, Haryana, India

First published in Penguin Enterprise by Penguin Random House India 2021

ISBN 9780670096206

Typeset in Adobe Caslon Pro
Printed at Replika Press Pvt. Ltd, India

www.penguin.co.in

To my beloved father

Captain Jack Shea

Contents

Contents

Introduction

Debora Ann Shea

I wanted to write this book a year after my father, Commodore Garnet Milton Shea, also known as 'Jack' Shea passed on. This is not only a tribute to his heroic role in saving a colleague and his family from almost certain elimination in a hostile country, it is also a humble salute to the unsung heroes who unflinchingly protect the honour, dignity and peace of our nation.

Dispossessed of parental love since birth, Jack grew up under the care of maternal grandparents, and with a name that belonged neither to his biological father or mother: 'Garnet Milton Shea.'

At seventeen, Jack Shea left his grandparents' house and joined the Royal Indian Navy. He lost his heart to a pretty young teacher, Dorothy Hope. They married and raised a wonderful family. His career blossomed.

A few months before the Indo–Pak war of 1965, Jack was posted to Karachi, Pakistan as Naval Attaché in the Indian High Commission, and here is where his story took a dramatic turn.

Prem Dewan, a First Secretary at the High Commission, was actually from the Indian Police Service. His role in sourcing vital military information during the 1965 Indo-Pak War brought him dangerously close to being booked for espionage. The Indian authorities knew they had to move quickly to get him and his family safely back to New Delhi.

The man assigned to head the mission: Jack Shea.

The ever-reliable Naval officer took on a task at which many had failed before. Charting out a route through precarious desert terrain, he set Prem Dewan on course for a safe escape. His meticulous planning ensured the Dewan family a safe passage by cargo ship.

Rattled and enraged, the ISI set out to identify the man behind the daring escape. After months of frustrating investigation, they finally had their man: Naval Attaché Captain Jack Shea.

Revenge was wreaked in the most brutal manner on a frosty January night, in the middle of a party inside the Indian Deputy High Commissioner's bungalow. Cornered and assaulted inside a toilet by four professional hitmen, Jack was thrown off the terrace and left for dead.

Badly battered, Jack lay comatose in a Karachi hospital for months, with little hope of survival. But no matter how broken in limb, his spirit remained uncrushed. Jack not only recovered but completed his tenure in Karachi and went on to receive two Ati Vishisht Seva Medals from the President of India. He assumed command of the Destroyer Squadron, played a pivotal role in the Indo–Pak War of 1971 and retired in 1976 as a Commodore.

I have captured as vividly as possible what I saw or experienced first-hand. The chapters on our move to Pakistan, the murderous assault on my father, his hospitalisation and the painful path to recovery, naval surveillance and house arrest are written through my experience and I affirm their authenticity. Other chapters are a creative narrative based on true events and reflect what I recall of all that I heard over the years from my family, especially my father and his friends. Some technical inaccuracies may have crept in due to the passage of time and the evolving scenario around me. I exhort the reader to try to relate to that epoch to enjoy the narrative.

Disclaimer

This book is a memoir, recreated by the Author upon her understanding of facts and events related to her by persons known to her. It reflects the Author's own understanding of the events recounted to her by various persons. Some names and places have been changed, some events have been compressed, and some dialogue has been recreated to suit the timelines and narrative of the book.

The objective of this book is not to hurt any sentiments or be biased in favour of or against any particular person, political party, region, caste, society, gender, creed, nation or religion.

Special Note

I would like to express my great appreciation for *Escape from Pakistan*. It has been Debbie's dream for five or six years to write and publish the story that her father narrated to her. The incident took place in Karachi when he was a diplomat in the Indian High Commission. She was unsure as to whether she would be able to do justice to the narration. However, I always encouraged her.

'You must,' I told her.

She took some time to research and stitch up the missing parts of the narrative. And she accomplished it. Truly, this is a work of passion. I wish her all the best in her venture.

Ravi Puravankara
Chairman, Puravankara Ltd

Foreword

My association with this book is the outcome of a conversation on another book written by a friend. I have known Debora for over a decade and have always admired her for her vast knowledge of history, politics and current affairs. A distinguished entrepreneur with varied interests, Debora has been an excellent mother, wife and friend.

We came to be acquainted through a common friend, my course mate from the National Defence Academy (NDA), who was adopted as a son by Admiral R L Pereira* in 1971 when he was the Deputy Commandant at the NDA. Admiral Pereira

---

* *Admiral R L Pereira PVSM AVSM was a Flag Officer in the Indian Navy. He served as the 10th Chief of Naval Staff from 1979 to 1982. He is considered to be one of the architects of the modern Indian Navy. He belonged to the Pereira family of Kannur, Kerala.*

and Jack Shea, the protagonist of this work were contemporaries and close family friends.

In 2018, my old friend Mike wrote a memorable book, "*The Admiral I Knew: A True Story of Admiral Ronald Lynsdale Pereira*"* where he recounts his journey with the Admiral from the day he adopted him till his demise. It is a sterling tribute to an exemplary officer and a gentleman, the finest role model, who profoundly impacted the growth of over 1,500 Officers of the Armed Forces trained under him at the NDA.

Debora informed me that she too was writing a book about her father and his times in the Navy with particular emphasis on his diplomatic tenure in Pakistan and would like me to read the manuscript. I thank Debora, the author of this book, for trusting me with her work and giving me a new mission in life.

Debora Shea's acerbic and factual account of her father's chutzpah, fortitude, trials and tribulations as Naval Attaché in Pakistan, and glorious innings in the Indian Navy is a beautiful voice to history with strength and courage. The candid retelling lends great vitality and power to the story of Jack Shea. Battered and bruised, Jack survives a fierce battle of life with innumerable constraints, yet courage and love defeat every challenge. A fascinating tale of how victimisation and violence are overcome with determination, faith, courage and the kind of resolve that some of us have been privileged to experience in our elders and the generation who came before us.

---

* *The Admiral I Knew: A True Story of Admiral Ronald Lynsdale Pereira* By Mike Bhalla, Vij Books (2018)

What sets *Escape from Pakistan* apart is the dexterity with which 'Principles of War' have been applied, upfront and subtly, in behind-the-scenes action, far away from the battlefield. A tribute to Jack Shea and all other gallant patriots who never flinch to protect the honour and security of their country, will certainly enthuse the men in uniform. I am certain it will appeal equally to others as a reminder of the sacrifices made by their brethren and encourage them to channelise their efforts towards nation building.

Debora has excelled in her first fling with writing and created a nice twisty story that has something for everyone; the historians, military practitioners, leaders, intellectuals and most of all for the romantics. A sweep-you-off-your-feet love narrative, effective suspense and diplomatic chicanery will keep the reader riveted and away from the haranguing news updates.

Air Marshal S P Singh
PVSM AVSM VM

Memories of My Friend Jack

I was closely associated with Commodore Garnet Milton Shea AVSM (Bar) from the early 1950s, popularly known to all his colleagues in the Navy as just 'Jack.' A calm, composed, dedicated officer who lived up to the credo 'Service before Self.'

During the 1965 conflict he was the Naval Attaché in Karachi. It was indeed trying times for all at the High Commission; Jack as usual rose to the occasion and weathered the storm.

On the occasion of the Naval Review by the President in 1974, Jack was The Review Commodore. The roaring success of The Presidential Review was entirely due to his meticulous planning and leadership, for which Jack was awarded a Commendation by The Chief of Naval Staff.

In 1967 Captain Shea was appointed Capt. D 11 of the 11th Destroyer Squadron (Rajput, Ranjit and Rana), a Command he carried out with professional elan and panache. The crest of Rajput is proudly displayed at the entrance of his house.

During his distinguished service in the Indian Navy, Jack proved his mettle and professional acumen time and time again and was awarded the Ati Vishisht Seva Medal in 1968, and the Bar to Ati Vishisht Seva Medal in 1972 for 'Distinguished Service'.

Jack retired in 1976.

Besides being a thorough professional, Jack had exemplary qualities of leadership and man management. He was popular with his subordinates not through populist measures but a genuine and sincere outreach. An incident I recall of his humane efforts at team building is when he joined the Shipping Corporation of India (SCI) on retirement. He, as Captain of M.V. Vishwa Parijat, organized a 'Bada Khaana' for the entire crew on Independence Day, onboard his ship, the first ever in the SCI.

It was an honour and privilege to closely associate with Jack, professionally and socially. Our children grew up together and we remained brothers in arms during our service in the Navy and post retirement.

Vice Admiral M R Schunker.
(Vice Chief of Naval Staff)
PVSM, AVSM Indian Navy [Retd]

1

The Attack on Jack

And how can man die better than facing fearful odds, for the ashes of his fathers, and the temples of his Gods.

—*Lord Macaulay**

26 January 1966. Karachi, Pakistan. Uma Bajpai, the Deputy High Commissioner of India in Pakistan, was hosting a party.

This Republic Day bore a special significance for India. In August 1965, the Indian Armed Forces had trounced the wily Pakistan President General Ayub Khan's troops, who had dared to attack India and challenge her sovereignty. Soon after, the Indian High Commission in Pakistan, despite heavy

---

* Thomas Babington Macaulay: From the poem *Lays of Ancient Rome*.

surveillance, had succeeded in repatriating one of its senior diplomats wanted for espionage in Pakistan.

On the surface, the invitation had been extended to offer foreign diplomats a window into Indian culture and cuisine. But the underlying message was hard to miss—this was a two-fold celebration: India's thumping success in the twenty-day war against Pakistan, followed by the successful escape of a senior diplomat and his family.

The front lawn of Uma Bajpai's palatial residence wore an exquisite look that evening. Prabha Amar Singh, wife of Amar Singh, First Secretary at the High Commission, was supervising the arrangements, as the Deputy High Commissioner was unmarried. She flitted busily about, adjusting a table runner here and instructing a bartender there. The fading glow of the setting sun gave way to the shimmer of the traditional earthen *diyas* (earthen oil lamps) lit in beautiful rows along the lawn borders and around fountains. The elegant setting of the large colonial bungalow was a sight to behold.

Barring a few, nobody knew that within a few hours, the scene would change from one of celebration to shock and horror.

Tulsi, the butler of the house, was the supply chain manager for the evening. As a large number of guests were expected, the Deputy High Commissioner had acceded to his request to hire four local helpers to ensure seamless service. The helpers had arrived early evening and Tulsi had taken them into his room in the servant's quarters, located towards the rear of the house.

Social gatherings in the diplomatic corps are planned with clockwork precision. The guests began to arrive by 7.00 p.m.

The ladies were resplendent in their traditional silken attire, with jewellery to match. The men were in black tie. The Naval Defence Attaché Captain Jack Shea, accompanied by his lovely wife Dorothy, arrived in his gleaming white Chevrolet. Their official driver, Muthu, was at the wheel. The Majordomo opened the car door and Jack alighted, impeccable in a tuxedo. Dorothy walked beside him, gorgeous in her peacock blue Kanjeevaram saree.

Amar Singh and Jack Shea were soon deep in conversation. Amar Singh was not drinking that night; he had a glass of water in his hand. Jack Shea was drinking Johnny Walker Black Label, his favourite 'poison,' and his glass was almost empty. Noticing this, Tulsi appeared by his side, bearing a tray.

Jack took a glass from the tray and thanked Tulsi for the prompt service. As Jack drank, still engaged in conversation, he suddenly started feeling dizzy and nauseous. Assuming it to be some innocuous discomfort, Jack gave his wife a gentle nudge and excused himself to go to the toilet.

Tulsi was waiting at the entrance to the house. He stepped forward. Jack put an unsteady hand on the butler's shoulder and asked to use the toilet. The butler walked him to the ground floor toilet, but it was locked.

'Sir, there is one on the first floor. Would you like to go there?'

Jack followed Tulsi upstairs, feeling increasingly unwell. He entered the toilet and turned to switch on the light when he sensed a movement close to him. Before he could react, a heavy object came crashing down on his head. As he swayed, another crack on the head accelerated his fall. Moments later, the full-blooded blow of a boot landed right in his face. Fading into unconsciousness, Jack curled into the foetal position, to reduce the effect of any further blows. He heard the toilet door open, followed by the sound of heavy boots striding in.

There seemed to be three or four men in the cramped toilet now. They repeatedly hit Jack, breaking every conceivable bone in his body. Relentless kicks in the ribs, despite the foetal position, caused blood to spurt from his mouth. The brutal assault didn't last long, as the assailants were trained to cause maximum damage in the shortest possible time.

Soon, Jack was unconscious—a lifeless heap of broken bones and bloodied skin. Their mission to kill him appeared to have been accomplished. However, to rule out any doubt, they picked him up, carried him to the terrace and flung him two floors down. He landed with a thud, between the sides of the bungalow and the compound wall.

Down in the lawns, the party was in full swing now. The Beatles were playing on the Deputy High Commissioner's Grundig music system. Dorothy, Jack's wife, was busy attending to the social obligations of a diplomat's wife and had not yet noticed Jack's long absence.

'Where's Jack, we don't see him,' asked a guest.

That's when Dorothy realized her husband had been away for over fifteen minutes. She started looking around but couldn't spot him. She rushed over to Amar Singh, who was engrossed in conversation with some US diplomats. She excused herself and whispered into Amar's ear.

'Amar, I can't see Jack anywhere. He went to the toilet about half an hour back. I'm getting really worried.'

Amar immediately put his glass down on the table and walked towards the house. He walked to the toilet on the ground floor, opened the door, and found it empty. He went to the pantry and asked the waiters if they had seen Jack; all responded in the negative.

That's when Amar Singh felt the first pangs of anxiety. He began searching from room to room but drew a blank everywhere until the sound of gushing water hit his ears on the first floor. He opened the toilet door and stared in shock—the washbasin was broken, and water was whooshing out of the broken pipe with full force. A wooden baton lay on the muddy floor, and blood was splattered all over, even on the walls.

This couldn't be good.

He rushed down the stairs directly to the Deputy High Commissioner and asked to have an urgent word with him.

Hearing what he had to say, Uma Bajpai immediately ordered the security to swing into action. A search party fanned out across the bungalow to look for the missing Naval Attaché.

The security guards confirmed that no car or vehicle had entered or exited in the last half hour. Amar sighed with relief; this meant that Jack was still on the premises—an abduction would have compounded the problem manifold. He ordered the gate to be locked and not opened under any circumstances.

A crucial thirty minutes had elapsed since the assault. Jack lay on the ground, broken and bleeding. He tried to move his battered limbs, but the seething pain allowed him only feeble moans before he relapsed into unconsciousness. Meanwhile, oblivious of the grim incident, the party carried on.

One of the waiters was walking back from the garden towards the bar to replenish his tray with drinks. He noticed the security guards running helter-skelter throughout the house. Out of sheer curiosity, he asked one of them, 'What happened, Sir?'

'Arrey! A guest had gone to the toilet over half an hour back and is untraceable since then. Have you seen or heard anything about Captain Saab?'

'No sir, I haven't seen him. But I thought I heard a strange sound at the rear of the house. Since I was busy serving the guests, I didn't get a chance to check what it was.'

'What did you hear?' one of the guards asked.

'I heard some kind of crying. Or groaning. It was quite low so I thought I might have imagined it.'

'Oh, my God. Where was it coming from?'

'That way,' he pointed. Then he put his tray down on the counter and led the guard toward the spot. Seeing them, the other guards followed.

The back of the house was a desolate patch, covered with overgrown plants and bushes. It lay in total darkness, but the low moans could still be heard in the quiet of the night. Somebody lit a torch, shone it into the thicket, and let out a shocked gasp. There lay Jack—bleeding profusely and obviously in intense pain.

The guards rushed to his side. Unaware of the battering the mangled mass had been subjected to, they tried to lift him up, inviting a blood-curdling scream that broke the eerie silence of the night. With utmost caution, they managed to shift him into one of the guest rooms on the ground floor.

Soon, Amar Singh reached the room where Jack had been laid down. By now, the entire household and the guests had sensed that something was amiss and rushed to see what had happened.

Amar Singh knelt by Jack's side and gently touched his crushed hand. 'What happened, Jack?'

Jack could barely open his badly bruised and swollen eyes, but managed to whisper, 'They were waiting in the bathroom . . . clobbered me . . . threw me off the terrace . . .'

Amar was at his wit's end and couldn't say anything except 'I'll get Dorothy, Jack. Just hold on,' and ordered one of the security guards to get her. He also instructed another staff of the house, 'Call the hospital and ask them to send an ambulance immediately.'

The guard rushed to get Dorothy, who by now had reached the entrance to the room. Fear gripped her as she saw the room packed with people and Amar Singh kneeling next to someone lying on the couch. She stood motionless; the breath trapped in her throat.

'What happened, Amar?' she murmured at last, daring to step forward. What she saw made her heart lurch—the man before her was a wreck: eyes swollen, nose skewed and bleeding, mouth lacerated, clothes torn, and the body covered in a gory mix of blood and mud.

'It's Jack,' said, Amar, softly. His words hit Dorothy like a ton of bricks.

'Oh, my God, how did this happen,' she wailed.

Amar steadied her somehow. Dorothy held Jack in a gentle embrace, her head resting close to his face. She cried, 'My love! My love! What have they done to you?'

Even in his semi-conscious state, Jack felt the comfort of his wife's affectionate embrace. A wave of relief washed over him. Mustering his diminishing strength, he whispered, 'I love you, sweetheart. Look after the children. I will be well and home soon.'

Soon the ambulance arrived, and the paramedics transferred Jack to the stretcher. Lying there, he pleaded, 'Amar, please look after . . .'

'Don't worry Jack, I'll take care of everything. I'll be there,' Amar Singh reassured him.

In his heart, Jack knew that the road to recovery was going to be long and treacherous. He began murmuring his favourite psalm: '*The Lord is my Shepherd* . . .'

No one paid any attention to Tulsi, who stayed in the background and watched the horror unfold. Seeing Jack, whom he had always respected, groan and gasp for every breath, he lamented 'Hey Ram! Yeh maine kya kar diya!' (Oh, God, what have I done!)

Amar and Dorothy accompanied Jack in the ambulance. It was late in the night, so most streets in Karachi were deserted, enabling the ambulance to reach the Seventh Day Adventist Hospital in less than fifteen minutes. The stretcher was wheeled into the Casualty Ward. Jack was unconscious by then. His heartbeat was feeble, breathing erratic and blood pressure dangerously low. The doctors wheeled him into the operation theatre. He would require multiple surgeries.

Within half an hour all guests from the party and the High Commissioner, G Parthasarathy, were at the hospital. Everyone was shocked at what had transpired.

Jack had been in the operation theatre for over three hours. Every passing moment felt like an eternity to Dorothy, who was desperately waiting to hear something comforting from the doctors. No amount of consolation provided any succour to her bleeding heart.

At last, the senior doctor emerged from the operation theatre, walked up to Dorothy and motioned her to come into the adjoining chamber. The High Commissioner and Amar Singh joined in. Dorothy sat there, steeling herself to hear what had happened.

'We have examined Mr Shea thoroughly. He has multiple fractures and injuries caused by blunt objects. The injury to the head is serious but we could not ascertain the damage, as he is unconscious. There is perforation of the lungs due to broken ribs, for which he has been put on oxygen support. Our preliminary assessment indicates that practically every bone in his body has suffered trauma in some form or the other. The heartening thing is that he is a young man with a strong heart. No cardiac trauma has been witnessed till now. The heart is beating rhythmically. There are no injuries to other vital organs. So, chances of recovery are there, but the probability of infection is very high due to extensive injuries. The patient is being kept in isolation to reduce the risk of infection and has been moved to the ICU in the Emergency Ward. His condition is extremely delicate, so only the medical staff and doctors are allowed to visit him till he stabilises. Please give him time to recover.'

With each word the doctor spoke, Dorothy felt her heart sink lower. All that she could comprehend was that Jack's injuries were not accidental but due to a brutal assault and that he was battling for life, with the scales heavily tilted against him.

It was well past midnight. The High Commissioner and other guests left after consoling Dorothy and assuring her of their full support. Amar chose to stay back with her, as nothing could convince her to leave the hospital. She sat on the bench outside the ICU, staring into oblivion, trying to come to terms with the horrific quirk of fate that had turned her beautiful life into a nightmare. Occasionally she would doze off and awaken with a start, shivering in the throes of an unkind and endless night.

2

Pakistan's Denial

Speak softly and carry a big stick; you will go far.

—*Theodore Roosevelt**

Soon after leaving the hospital, High Commissioner G. Parthasarathy called up the Defence Minister and briefed him about the assault on the Naval Attaché. He was advised to meet the Foreign Minister of Pakistan and convey India's concerns in unequivocal terms. He was also advised to take up the matter with the Russian Ambassador, who had been instrumental in brokering the truce during the Indo-Pak war.

Life-threatening injuries inflicted on an Indian diplomat, purportedly by Pakistani agents, in an Indian diplomats'

---

* Theodore Roosevelt: quoting a West African proverb.

residential area, was a serious breach of protocol and a violation of the immunity granted under the Geneva Convention.

Pakistan tried upending the incident, terming it a self-inflicted injury incurred in an inebriated state. But India was not buying that narrative.

The Pakistani High Commissioner was summoned to the office of the Minister of External Affairs in New Delhi, and India's deep concern was conveyed to him with a warning of reciprocal action, should Pakistan fail to bring to book the culprits. It was nothing short of a 'pack your bags and leave' message. The Pakistani High Commissioner, who was totally unaware of the incident, was speechless. He assured the External Affairs Minister that he would convey India's concerns to his Government. He left the South Block, wearing a lugubrious look.

In Karachi, the Indian High Commissioner sought and was granted an appointment with Zulfikar Ali Bhutto, Foreign Minister of Pakistan. They had met on a cordial note once, well before the Indo-Pak war, when he had presented his credentials to the President on assuming charge as India's High Commissioner. This, however, was going to be an awkward meeting.

Parthasarathy was ushered into the Minister's office. Bhutto got up from his chair to welcome him.

'Good morning High Commissioner. How are you?' He offered a firm handshake and gestured to him to take a seat across the table.

'Good morning, Sir, thank you very much for your time.'

'What can I get you? Tea or coffee?'

'Just a glass of water will be fine, Sir,' replied Parthasarathy.

'So, what brings you here?'

'Sir, this is somewhat unpleasant, but I have come to convey the profound concerns of the Government of India about a serious assault inflicted on our Naval Attaché by some Pakistani citizens at a diplomatic party in the Deputy High Commissioner's residence. The officer was beaten mercilessly and thrown off the terrace of the building by a group of people. He is lying in the hospital, in a coma, hanging precariously between life and death. I might reiterate that as per the United Nations Charter it is the responsibility of the Pakistani Government to ensure the safety and protection of the Indian personnel working in the High Commission.'

Bhutto, already briefed about the incident by his Chief of Internal Security, put on a charade of shock.

'That's not possible, not in my country. I'm sure there is some serious misunderstanding, High Commissioner. Anyway, I'm really sorry to hear about this incident. We will set up a committee to investigate and go to the root of the matter.' After a short pause, he repeated, 'This is not possible, not in my country,' in a tone that betrayed overbearing confidence.

'I am afraid Sir, we may have run the course of patience and understanding in this matter. God forbid the officer loses his life, it will be an act of war, a serious violation of the Tashkent Agreement, and the Government of Pakistan will be guilty of travesty of the treaty signed a few months back.'

'Be assured High Commissioner, this cannot be the case. There must be some error in the information you have. I am certain that there has not been nor will ever be a contravention of any charter or treaty signed between our two countries.'

'I hope so. But I have serious reservations, especially in view of the fact that your country has often violated the 1961 Vienna Convention on Diplomatic Relations and held us hostage in the High Commission for three days and our families in our residences in Hindustan Court/ Shivaji Court for weeks on end. And I am here to register our Government's serious objection to such perfidy by Pakistan.'

'Let me assure you, High Commissioner, we had no intention to hold you hostage. We had to protect the High Commission, your staff, and your families from the angry mobs that wanted to attack you. You may recall that the US Embassy in Moscow was attacked by angry mobs in March this year and it took a Herculean effort to quell the violence. We did not want the situation to go out of hand and took pre-emptive action to ensure your safety by securing your areas with army troops. In fact, I was expecting a word of thanks and appreciation from you and your Ministry; on the contrary, you are belittling us for ensuring your safety. Anyway, I shall look into the matter at the earliest.'

'Kindly take serious cognizance of this incident. My government will deeply appreciate it if our concerns are conveyed to your President. I'll take your leave, Sir. Good day.'

High Commissioner Parthasarathy got up to leave. Mr Bhutto too rose from his chair, shook the High Commissioner's hand, rang the bell and asked his assistant to escort the High Commissioner to the door.

3

The Rann Bankure: Men of Steel

Build me a son, O Lord, who will be strong enough to know when he is weak, and brave enough to face himself when he is afraid; one who will be proud and unbending in honest defeat, and humble and gentle in victory.

*—General Douglas McArthur** *

Four weeks had passed. Jack lay comatose in the ICU at the Seventh Day Adventist Hospital. Doctors could give no assurance on his chances of recovery due to the serious head injury he had suffered. But there was a silver lining. His physical parameters were improving, thanks to his strong sports-trained

---

* General Douglas Macarthur: From *A Father's Prayer*.

body. Before the assault, he had been in the pink of health— he was a boxer in school and played hockey for the Navy.

The lungs were the first to show signs of improvement. Jack started breathing normally and was weaned off the oxygen. Gradually, the concussion and hematoma also began to subside.

Dorothy spent most of her waking time at the hospital, praying for Jack's recovery. She also took good care of her two young children and the newly born infant. Ladies from the High Commission were always at hand to help her with homemade food and comforting words.

Even so, the prolonged dark saga left Dorothy wilting under the strain. Never had she in the weirdest of nightmares imagined that the love of her life would lie comatose, and she would be helpless. Over the years, she had grown accustomed to Jack's solid, loving presence. She lost her appetite and grew irritable. She would spend most of the time sitting outside the ICU, watching Jack through the glass window, and solving the crossword in the newspapers. She tried keeping the faith that 'anything that's long divided, will surely unite.'

Day Thirty. Dorothy sat outside the ICU, a gentle smile playing on her lips. A kaleidoscope of sweet memories was streaming through her mind. She remembered their first meeting, his nonchalant 'Jack for Doe and Doe for Jack' catchphrase that had initially riled her but later became their most cherished one-liner. Rides on the Marine Drive with Jack on his beloved motorcycle, their wedding in England, the birth of their first son . . .

Suddenly, the Duty Nurse came bolting out of the ICU and rushed towards her. 'Ma'am! The Captain has regained consciousness!'

The nurse's words, like a benediction from the Almighty, shook Dorothy out of her reverie. She clutched the nurse's hand and ran to Jack's bedside.

'Boo!' she called out, as she always used to do.

Jack opened his eyes and saw Dorothy leaning over him, her eyes welling up with tears. He reached for her hand. She clasped his stretched hand in both hers. Jack's lips quivered. Dorothy thought she heard 'Doe,' but his eyes shut again. She stood there transfixed, tears streaming down her cheeks. She sensed Jack's fingers move between her hands and knew he had won the battle for survival. 'Thank you, God. Thank you so much,' she murmured.

The Duty Doctor was informed by the nurse. As he walked in, he saw Dorothy holding Jack's hand. He gave her a gentle smile and called out, 'Jack! How are you feeling?'

A twitch on Jack's face and a slight movement of his fingers assured the doctor that he was coming around. He checked his vitals, had a word with the nurse, gave Dorothy another reassuring smile and left the ICU.

As the Duty Doctor left, Dr Maria D'Souza held Dorothy's hand, caressed it and whispered, 'He's turned the corner, my dear!' Dorothy was speechless. Standing there, she realized how lonely and miserable she had been since Jack's accident, with no one to share her pain. The children were too young and her sisters too far away in India. She hugged Dr D'Souza, put her head on her shoulder, and let the tears flow. The doctor ushered her gently outside the ICU and sat with her till Dorothy regained her composure.

Regaining consciousness made Jack aware of all the frailties of his medical condition. He experienced excruciating pain every time he moved. The searing temperature made him delirious as he drifted in and out of consciousness. From time to time, he murmured 'Baba!' seeking solace in his father's memory. The path to recovery was not easy. The brutality of the assault had left Jack with far too many injuries and broken limbs and bones. His legs, hips, knees, ankles, wrists, shoulders, and elbows had suffered fractures; he had torn ligaments and muscular trauma. His memory appeared to be intact, though. He opened his eyes now and then, and responded through gestures, as he was yet to regain speech. But nobody was complaining about the slow pace of healing—they all knew that his survival was nothing short of a miracle. A few days later, Jack was moved from the ICU to a private room in the hospital.

The High Commissioner and Deputy High Commissioner visited the hospital frequently to check up on Jack's health. The High Commissioner spoke with the attending doctor.

'Let me assure you, High Commissioner, you are witnessing nothing short of a miracle. When he came in a month ago, his physical condition indicated a curtain call for him,' said the doctor. 'But his indomitable spirit and steely resolve have pulled him back from the precipice. He is no ordinary man.'

'No doubt about that, Doctor,' said the High Commissioner. 'He has the blue blood of a Rajput, the Rann Bankuras, coursing through his veins.' As he left, he added, 'Thank you, Doctor, for all the care and support. We are grateful to you.'

Soon, Jack was alone. The words '*Blue blood of a Rajput, Rann Bankura,*' kept echoing in his mind, taking him back to the proud legacy so often narrated to him by his father,

Mahendra Singh. He wistfully remembered his times with his father, their special bond, and his being an anchor in an ocean of uncertainty . . .

* * *

It was well past eight in the morning on 23 March 1923. Saroo, the zamindar's driver, was waiting at the Agra railway station for the train coming from Bombay. As it chugged in, Saroo rushed to the first-class compartment and bowed to his Master's only son as he stepped off the train.

Mahendra Singh, a strapping young lad of nineteen, the scion of the Rajput family of Chauhans, was returning home after completing his graduation in London. The Chauhans were wealthy landlords of Agra. Rajputs, the 'sons of kings', of whom every man was a dauntless kshatriya and every woman a heroine, were a clan distinguished for their military ardour. Saroo ushered him to the gleaming white Rolls-Royce Phantom parked outside the railway station.

'Thakur Sahib has bought this car for you from Delhi,' said Saroo, starting the engine. Mahendra scanned the stunning interiors of this latest offering from Rolls-Royce: its plush interiors, the almost inaudible hum of the engine and the comfortable seating.

They passed a group of teenage girls, walking to school. Suddenly, a raven-haired beauty with milky white skin, emerald eyes, and a charming smile, caught Mahendra's eye. Enchanted by her daisy-fresh looks, he asked, 'Who is that girl, Saroo? The girl in the blue frock.'

Saroo slowed down the car and adjusted the rear-view mirror to catch a glimpse of the girls.

'Hazoor, she is Gladys, the daughter of the Postmaster General, a British Sahib.'

'Can we stop for a while,' he asked the driver.

'We could, Sahib, but Thakur Sahib has been impatiently waiting for you for last so many days. Let us come back tomorrow,' replied Saroo.

Mahendra nodded, and sighed to himself, 'What a beauty!'

The very next day, Mahendra drove by where he had first seen Gladys. Lo and behold! The same group of girls was walking to school. He asked Saroo to park the car on the side of the road and walked towards them.

'Hello! I'm Mahendra Singh. May I drop you to your school in my car?'

'We are going to St Peter's School. It's not very far and we are quite used to walking. Thank you for your kind offer,' said one of the girls. They all exchanged looks and giggled.

'Oh well! Then if you don't mind, I shall walk along with you,' he said, and fell in step beside Gladys.

The girls tittered daintily. Mahendra was a good-looking lad and they were happy to have him walk along. One of them said, 'By the way, I am Susan, she is Martha, that is Mary, this is Litty, and next to you, the gorgeous Gladys.'

'Hello everyone!' said Mahendra.

Soon, they reached the school and parted company.

'What time does the school get over? I can pick you up . . .' he offered.

But the girls skipped away happily, without giving him a reply.

Mahendra was smitten by the beautiful English rose, Gladys. He lay awake at night, unable to get her out of his mind. Her beauty haunted him.

Saroo had already found out that the school got over at 4.00 p.m. So, the next day, he was ready with the car at 3.30 p.m. and by 4.00 p.m., Mahendra Singh was outside the school gate. He leaned against the car, waiting for the girls. Gladys was the first to come out. She saw young Mahendra in a light-blue Burberry trench with a scarf to match, every inch the Adonis. She couldn't take her eyes off him.

As he saw the girls come out of the gate, he walked towards them.

'Hello! It's so nice to see you all.'

Susan giggled, 'You are standing outside our school. Of course, you are here to see us.'

Mahendra smiled at her coquettish repartee, 'You are so cheeky, Sweety,' said Mahendra with a charming smile.

'Shall we drive in my car or would you prefer to walk? Promise I will show you some beautiful places in this quaint town of ours.'

'Ooooooh!' There was a collective sigh.

Driving in a Rolls-Royce Phantom car in the 1920s, in a small principality like Agra, was a mark of one's arrival among the few 'high and mighty.'

Saroo stopped the car outside the park. Everyone got out of the car to walk around the lawns. Gladys dropped back a little. She half-turned and gave Mahendra a smile. Mahendra's heart skipped a beat; this sudden pearly windfall seemed too much to bear. He gathered his wits, smiled back at Gladys, and hastened his pace to walk alongside her.

'You have very beautiful eyes. I could drown in them,' he whispered.

Gladys blushed and ran away.

Mahendra looked skywards and sighed. Cupid's arrow had struck the bullseye. For the next few weeks, Mahendra and Saroo would pick up the girls for school and also drop them home after school. The trips to and from school were fun and they all looked forward to it.

Mahendra's cousins were visiting from the neighbouring states, so he decided to host a high tea party. He invited the girls to his house, and also some friends, who were visiting from the university in England.

Gladys looked luscious in a powder pink frock. Mahendra joined the group where she was standing. He moved closer to her.

'Let me show you the family portraits. Come with me,' he whispered.

She followed him as if she was hypnotized.

They walked into the house, and he led her upstairs to the first floor.

Mahendra opened a hall with magnificent chandeliers. There were large portraits hanging all along the walls. Mahendra pointed at the portraits of his grandfather, father, his mother, and grandmother.

'How majestic and royal,' cooed Gladys, fascinated by the grandeur of it all as they moved along the gallery, and overawed by the young handsome man walking next to her. A tender and warm feeling, never experienced before, enveloped and confused her.

Mahendra who had continuously been explaining things to her, suddenly sensed that she was in a daze, and her beautiful green eyes were transfixed on him. He stopped speaking mid-sentence and moved closer to her.

He looked down into the green pools of her eyes and found himself drowning. He was inches away from her and could feel her breath, the haunting fragrance of the English rose, all over him. Her heart was racing and so was his. He reached for her hand, pulled her closer and put his arm around her, and embraced her gently, not knowing what to do next. And then under the pre-ordained blessings of his ancestors, he bent his head to touch her lips with his. The softness of her lips and the warmth of her embrace sent an electrifying shock down his spine. It was a moment filled with ecstasy and desire as their embrace tightened, seeking more of each other. He held her tight, every inch of their bodies rapturously intertwined. Mahendra was aroused with the passion of a nineteen-year-old. He kissed her repeatedly and passionately. She clung to him with a divine feeling she had never felt before. They were in a trance, lost in their own world of discovery.

'Mahendra!' Someone called out aloud.

'Mahendra!!'

'Mahendra!!!'

It was the third hail in the familiar baritone of the zamindar that pierced through their bliss. Mahendra didn't want to let go of Gladys. The nectar of her soft lips and her angelic embrace had elevated him to the seventh heaven, a sensation unfamiliar to him. He turned towards the door holding Gladys, a storm raging in his heart and mind. He gently released his hold on her after repeatedly kissing her and walked out of the room and closed the door softly behind him.

Gladys was thoroughly confused at what had just happened. Her face was flushed pink and her heart in a riot. As she composed herself, she felt ecstatic and gentle love for Mahendra's chutzpah.

After that day, they met every day after school, in a hunting lodge on the outskirts of Mahendra's family estate. One day, driven by wild, erotic passion both of them decided to elope to Meerut where Mahendra's cousin lived. Mahendra told his father that he was going to Meerut to visit his cousin Ranjit, while Gladys convinced her mother that she was going on a three-day excursion with her friends. They stayed in one of Ranjit Singh's family guesthouses in Meerut. A day later they got married in a simple ceremony at a local temple.

It was not long before Mahendra's father, the Thakur got wind of his son's escapades. He was furious. He sent his people and a senior official to convince Mahendra to return to Agra, with instructions to escort Gladys to her father's house with due respect. She was an English girl, so they could not afford to upset the British officials. It was a volatile situation that needed careful handling.

Within a week, Mahendra was sent away to England for further studies. The blossoming love of the teenagers was nipped in the bud. Mahendra and Gladys were separated, never to meet again.

Over the weeks and months, Gladys nursed a broken heart, weeping incessantly. She barely left her room. Her friends would come over to visit her, but she would sit quietly and not say a word. Everybody had heard about Mahendra and Gladys's love story. They all felt sad that it had ended so tragically.

Soon, Gladys's mother Henrietta, to her utter dismay, discovered that young Gladys was with child. She couldn't reconcile to the fact that her daughter was carrying the child of an Indian and informed her husband, George Carmen, about Gladys's pregnancy. He was livid that his daughter was involved in a romantic escapade with the local landlord's son. This would stir up a storm in the British circles.

George visited the Thakur at the manor. He was accorded the due courtesy befitting a British officer of the Raj. But when he brought up Gladys, the Thakur blatantly denied the whole affair. He said he had no knowledge of a liaison between his son and Gladys, and informed George that Mahendra had returned to England for higher studies, after his betrothal to the daughter of a landlord from Meerut. The marriage was to be solemnized soon after he returned from England.

George Carmen seethed with anger, as he could clearly discern the zamindar's lies. But he was helpless, as there was really nothing he could do. He returned home, crestfallen. He was deeply disappointed in his daughter and determined to set things right for her future.

George and Henrietta tried their utmost to convince Gladys to abort the child. But abortions were in their nascent stage in those days and extremely dangerous for the mother, so Gladys refused. She was sure of her love and firmly believed that Mahendra would return to her. Alas! It was not to be. There was no word from Mahendra or his family.

Gladys delivered a premature baby boy in the seventh month of her pregnancy. Diminutive in size and fragile in health, the baby was tiny enough to sleep in a cigar box. It was only due to vigilant nursing and Henrietta's motherly care that he survived.

To overcome the sad saga of family betrayal and the attendant ignominy that stared George Carmen in the face, Gladys was married off to a young Irish man, Michael Thomas Shea. George sent them away to Bombay to start a new life.

The little boy remained with his grandparents in their home. George named him Jack and appointed a nanny and a manservant, Eddy, to look after him. His grandparents provided all the love, care, and nurturing of a parent. Jack too was very attached to his grandparents.

Jack and Eddy would walk to Day School every day. Jack's best friend was a squirrel that Eddy caught for him in the garden. Jack made a cosy home for the squirrel in a shoe box, lined with old woollen rags. He also had a dog called 'Red,' a cocker spaniel, with a rusty red coat and soft brown eyes. Normally Red lay in the veranda and waited for Jack to return from school. As soon as he saw Eddy open the gate, he knew Jack had returned and would come bounding towards him. Jack would bend down and cuddle him. He had two budgerigars in a cage that his grandfather had bought him for his birthday. Jack loved filling up their bowls with bird seed and water every day, and clean up the nests, once every few days.

Jack loved the evenings, especially dinner time, as he got an opportunity to sit in his grandfather's lap and eat his dinner.

Grandfather would tuck him into bed and sit next to him, reading a bedtime story till he was lulled into sleep. Jack loved his beautiful and private world as a child.

However, his cradle of comfort was to be viciously rocked a week after his fourth birthday. A Ford car drove up to the Carmen's bungalow. Out stepped a handsome man, holding a huge bouquet of pink English roses and the hope of reuniting with his lost love, Gladys.

'Good afternoon, Sir. I am Mahendra Singh,' he said to George, who looked the same except for the gently receding hairline.

'Good day to you. Though I have never been introduced to you, I am aware of you. Several years ago, I had gone to meet your father at the manor. He told me that you had no troth with Gladys and were betrothed to a zamindar's daughter from Meerut before you returned to England to complete your education.'

'I apologise, Sir! That is a dastardly untruth. I was too young then to decide on anything for myself. Gladys and I were in love, we had eloped and married. I wanted to come and seek your blessings but the moment my father learnt about our liaison, he locked me up and sent me away to England, despite my pleas and protests. My father thought that was in the best interest of the family. But now that I am back and standing on my own feet, I want to be with Gladys. Please allow me to meet her; I am dying to see her and honour my troth to her. I realize that my naivety has caused you and the family a great deal of pain, especially to Gladys. I am here to make amends and seek your blessings, and I assure you Sir that Gladys has always been and will forever be the queen of my heart. Please, Sir, forgive me and give us a chance.'

'The least you could have done was to communicate with me or Gladys. I was aghast, and Gladys was heartbroken at your silence, so I believed whatever your father told me. It has caused me and the family considerable distress.'

'I was helpless, Sir. My father had threatened to harm Gladys if I ever communicated with her or with you. I didn't want any harm to come your way.'

'Well son, it's too late now,' George said, quietly. 'Five years is too long for a young girl to wait for someone, and to live with the blemish of jilted love. I had to save my daughter from scandal and dishonour, so I married her off to an English gentleman. I trust for the sake of your love and her life you will not disturb her in any manner. She has endured enough misery for one lifetime.'

Mahendra was devastated. The beautiful bouquet of English roses dropped out of his hands, along with his dreams of starting life afresh with Gladys. He had endured five years in the bone-chilling winters of England, dreaming of Gladys, reminiscing over the beautiful days they spent together and planning his future life with her. And now, his dreams had come crashing in one fell swoop.

As he finished speaking, George heard Red bounding towards the gate. Jack had returned from school. As Jack entered the house, he saw his grandfather in the living room speaking with a stranger. He ran to him, to give his grandfather the customary hug. George gave Jack a big hug.

Something came over George and he muttered, 'Mahendra, he is your boy,' pointing towards Jack.

Mahendra was thunderstruck. He never imagined such a twist of fate. It broke his heart to think that Gladys had to go through all the misery and sorrow of carrying and delivering a child, without ever being able to admit who the father was. How hard it must have been on her.

'Oh, God! What have I done?' he lamented, sobbing uncontrollably, head hung in sorrow. George waited for Mahendra to compose himself and put a hand on his drooping shoulders. Jack, somewhat confused, stood next to his grandfather, holding his hand. Mahendra got down on his knee and gazed at the boy, tears glimmering in his eyes. He held him close for a long time and murmured 'Kunwar sa!'

While Eddy was tidying the living room the next day, he gathered the bouquet that lay on the floor. A white envelope lying on the table caught his eye. He picked it up and gave it to George, who opened it even though it was addressed to Gladys.

* * *

28 May 1928.

My Sweet Gladys,

Forgive me for the long passage of time. Trust me, the days were as long for me as they have been for you. But I carried you in my heart every day, hoping one day to come back and see you again.

A gentle tap on my shoulder,
And I turned around
An entire world that was hidden in the shadows

Eons ago
Opens up in a myriad of ways
And
I remember the depths of your eyes
The smile on your lips
I could feel the love you had carried within
But could never say
The touch of your hand
And the warm embrace
I've walked so many hapless miles
Fought so many battles on my own
With never a hug
Never a kiss
To help me along
A gentle nudge
A shoulder to rest on.
We are thousands of miles away
So distant
So apart
And yet the soul over stretching to you
Can I reach you
Can I touch you
Let me feel again
Let me live again
It'll always be you
It'll always be for you
Though reason and thought overtake me
I believe one day when it's all done
I'll turn to you

You'll return to me
One touch of your hand
And you'll restore my soul
It'll be ok
I'm sure it'll be ok

Yours eternally,
Mahendra

* * *

George folded the letter with a moist eye. His heart reached out to his hapless daughter and the devoted young man. A love so tender should never have been lost. He slid the letter into the drawer of his writing-table. He buried the letter. He buried their love.

In the early twentieth century, marriages in feudal households were arranged by the elders, to whom amicable relations between the families mattered more than the sentiments of the bride and the groom. Despite being educated in England, Mahendra had no choice but to marry into a zamindar family of Meerut, just as his father had ordained five years back.

Mahendra never struck a chord with his wife. They remained cordial but detached, with no marital intimacy. He clung to his son and the memories of his lost love, Gladys. He started to frequent Carmen House regularly to visit his son, showering him with gifts and love. Jack began to look forward to his father's visits. As soon as the car pulled up, he would run to the gate and squeal 'Baba' with delight as Mahendra took him in his arms and twirled him around. Joining in the fun, Red would leap high into the air. Henrietta, Jack's grandmother, grew worried about the growing affection between father and son.

Mahendra was well aware that despite his growing affection for his son, he could never take him back to his house, especially as his wife remained childless. After a year, Mahendra set up a fund for Jack's education in La Martiniere College, Lucknow. It was an educational institution for the children of the British gentry and elite Indian families. Mahendra wanted his son to have the best education available in India.

George accepted Mahendra's offer to support Jack's school education but made it abundantly clear that the boy would never carry Mahendra's name, either in his school records or thereafter. Accepting the circumstances with grace, Mahendra promised to stay incognito in matters related to his son.

With the solitary stumbling block out of the way, George drew up the papers for Jack to be adopted by his son-in-law Michael Shea. And so, Jack, a scion of the Rajput bloodline, was christened 'Garnet Milton Shea.' One can only imagine how deep it cut Mahendra Singh, but the man stayed true to his word.

At ten, Jack was admitted into the prestigious La Martiniere College, Lucknow. He returned to Agra for the summer and winter holidays. Mahendra, meanwhile, began spending more of his time in England, away from an unsuccessful marriage and haunting memories of Gladys. The meetings between father and son became less frequent, as a result.

Jack met his mother, Gladys, once a year at Christmas when she visited her parents. Every year that the Shea family came to visit the Carmens, there would be a new addition to their family. Jack grew fond of his half-sister Elvina. She was closer in age to him and loved to play with him in the fields and the gardens.

But deep down in his heart, he did not view them as his family. For him, his little world revolved around his grandfather and grandmother. Over the years, in the absence of his parents, Jack would often feel a lingering sense of loneliness. But his was destined to be a life of grit and valour, as the coming years would amply prove.

4

Jack Meets His Doe

All power is within you; you can do anything and everything.

—*Swami Vivekananda*[*]

The years flew by. Jack turned seventeen and completed his Intermediate Certificate. An avid reader of history books, especially naval campaigns, he also loved classical music and wrote short stories and poems.

Once Grandpa came home, he would settle him in his rocking chair. Eddy would bring his slippers and a cup of hot tea. Jack would chat with his grandfather until dinner was served. The three of them would sit at the table and eat their dinner. This remained a family ritual from the time Jack could sit on his grandfather's lap to the day he left home.

---

[*] Swami Vivekananda: Lectures from Colombo to Almora.

One such evening, Jack sat next to his grandfather, who was cleaning his pipe. He ventured, 'Grandpa, I have been reading extensively about the Royal Navy. I find it very exciting and would like to join.'

Grandpa peered at Jack with his kindly eyes. Then he said, 'Yes Jack, a career in the Royal Navy sounds interesting, but all naval ports are on the coastline, far away from here. Besides, we want you to pursue higher studies and take up a job closer home.'

'I know, Grandpa! I too don't want to go away from you—I love you and Grandma dearly. But then I do want to make a career in the Royal Navy. I have seen photographs of officers in uniforms. They look really smart and distinguished.'

'Well! I'm sorry to disappoint you, son, but Gran and I wish for you to study medicine and become a doctor. I have written to the King Albert Memorial Hospital in England. Once they reply, we shall apply for your admission to the Medical College.'

Jack gazed beseechingly at his grandfather, but George was unmoved. Jack knew that repeating his request would be like whistling in a gale, yet he tried again and then again. George wouldn't relent, leaving Jack in a deep dilemma. His grandparents meant the world to him, but he couldn't reconcile to the idea of spending his entire life in Lucknow or Agra. He would be like a bird in a gilded cage and that surely was not for him.

The truth was, Jack had already applied to the Royal Navy before speaking with his grandfather. He had also begun saving up to leave. Besides money, he had put away some clothes and toiletries in a knapsack and packed a woollen blanket in a holdall and hid them away, especially from Eddy, who was sure to squeal to Grandpa if he knew.

Jack waited impatiently for a call letter from the Navy for the entrance examination in Bombay. He knew what time to expect the postman and would wait at the door to collect the mail. During the day, he spent all his time helping his grandmother around the house. This was the least he could do for her, as she had devoted her life to bring him up and ensure his wellbeing. He wanted to be there for her in her sunset years. Occasionally, the thought of leaving her and the uncertainty of his return made him feel downcast.

Five weeks after he had filed his application, Jack received a letter from the Royal Navy asking him to report to Bombay and sign up for the entrance examination. Jack was ecstatic but didn't share the information with anyone. He went to the railway station and bought himself a ticket on a direct train to Bombay, scheduled to leave after two days. The next day he was pensive, filled with guilt at leaving his grandparents, and went to bed with a heavy heart.

The train to Bombay left early, so he got up before dawn, had a hearty breakfast, and asked the cook to pack some sandwiches for him. 'Tell Grandpa that I'll be out for the day,' he told the cook. As he left, he turned around one last time, locked the gate, and walked away.

The journey to Bombay took two days and was quite comfortable. Jack made his way to the address on the letter from the Navy. The reception clerk gave him the details for the examination, which was to be held two days later.

Although his mother and foster father lived in Bombay, Jack did not want to stay with them. During the day, he spent hours in a public library, preparing for the examination. In the evening, he sat on the benches at Cuffe Parade, watching the ships sail in and out of the harbour. At night, he slept in the waiting room at the railway station.

Jack cleared the examination with ease and joined the Indian Naval Volunteer Reserve as a Midshipman in 1942. The following year, he was commissioned as an acting Sub-Lieutenant.

After the Commissioning ceremony, Jack stayed back at the Docks. One evening, he sat down to pen a letter to his grandparents. The Sub-Lieutenant epaulettes adorned his shoulders, their golden hue reflecting his pride and joy. He wrote about all that he had been through since he had left them. He thanked them for all the love and care they had bestowed on him and apologised profusely for not writing to them earlier and leaving the house unannounced. He told them that he missed them badly but was very happy as he had accomplished his resolve to join the Navy and was now a Commissioned officer, a Midshipman, in the Royal Indian Navy.

* * *

16 June 1944

Darling Grandpa and Grandma,

You are the first one I want to share my news with. Today was the Commissioning Ceremony. I became a Commissioned officer in the Royal Indian Navy. I am a Sub Lieutenant now. I just wanted to thank you and Grandma for all the love and care you have given me and made me into whoever I am today. I came away nearly two years ago. I didn't have the heart to tell you. I didn't want to disappoint you. I hope you are not disappointed in me. I just wanted to join the Navy. I'll write a letter to Baba also. Please give it to him when he comes to visit you. And thank him for everything. He knew that I was keen to join the Navy. And always encouraged me to follow my dreams.

I snuck away quietly. And I came to Bombay and appeared for the Entrance Exam to the Royal Indian Navy. I passed the exam and got inducted into the forces. I am now doing my training at the Naval Dockyard in HMIS Dalhousie. And our accommodation is in Dhanraj Mahal, near the Gateway of India. It is quite comfortable, and there are a lot of chaps with me. We all stay in a large dormitory, with rows and rows of beds, tables, and lockers for our things. It's still early days and everything is very exciting.

But I miss you Grandpa, and Grandma too. I'm happy. Don't worry about me. As soon as I get some weeks off, after my training is done, I'll come back to Agra to visit you. Please give my love to Grandma. Give Red a big hug, and Eddy also.

Please look after yourself.

I love you dearly.

Your loving grandson,
Jack

* * *

George Carmen was overwhelmed. He wrote back promptly, congratulating his beloved grandson and sending him a cheque of three thousand rupees for Jack to buy himself a motorcycle. As soon as he received the letter, Jack went to a motorcycle showroom in Colaba and bought himself the popular, red-coloured Indian Chief Motorcycle, the envy of all young officers. He took a photograph sitting on the motorcycle and sent it to his grandfather. He enjoyed riding around with his friends, as it burnished his handsome persona, and was quite the man about town.

The Navy became his life and passion. A diligent and disciplined sailor, Jack excelled in every field of activity and was soon promoted to the rank of Lieutenant.

Sunday was a weekly off, so the young officers would eagerly await Saturday evening to get together and have fun. Jack had dated some girls from time to time without any serious commitment. Then one fine evening, Cupid struck.

It was a Saturday. A classmate of Jack from La Martiniere days invited him for his birthday party at the United Services Club, in Colaba. Jack accompanied his friend Mazhar Khan to the party. He wore his newly acquired navy-blue pinstripes jacket and looked dashing, reminiscent of his father Mahendra.

It was a lively gathering of over fifty, including some naval friends. As the golden hits of Frank Sinatra, the king of 'Swooner Crooner' era, began to play, young couples moved to the floor. Jack was looking around for a partner, when he saw four young men speaking to one another and a pretty lady standing next to them. She seemed somewhat forlorn. Jack walked up to her and realized she was far more beautiful than she looked from a distance. 'Hello, I am Jack, a Lieutenant in the Navy,' he said. 'I am here at the invitation of my friend, Soares.'

'Oh!' said Dorothy. Though known for her ready wit and vivacity, Dorothy was a bit startled at this sudden encounter with a stranger. 'I am Doe,' she managed. 'Dorothy Hope. I am a teacher at the Cathedral and John Connon School.'

'That's a very pretty name, Doe!' said Jack. 'And 'Hope' gives me oodles of hope that we can do great things together. So, it will be Doe for Jack and Jack for Doe!' What do you say?'

Dorothy couldn't believe her ears. Everything around her seemed to freeze. She shook her head.

'Watch it, I have a boyfriend,' she lied.

Jack was too smitten to take cognisance of what she said.

'Oh, so you want a Coke,' he blurted and before she could open her mouth. He was gone.

Dorothy came from a family that traced its ancestry to Oliver Henry Bensley, the Superintendent of Police for the Madras Constituency that encompassed the entire southern part of the Indian subcontinent. In 1902, Bensley was appointed the first trustee of 'The Club Trivandrum' after the erstwhile 'European Club,' patronised only by the English elite, was rechristened. Over the years, he developed a strong friendship with the Maharaja of Travancore, Sree Moolam Thirumal. The Maharaja was inducted as the first Indian member of this Club, opening the doors of membership to select aristocrats and elites of Indian origin.

The Maharaja exhorted Bensley to start a bank in Travancore. In deference to his wishes, Oliver Bensley founded

'The Bank of Travancore' and worked closely with the Maharaja to manage his wealth.

Oliver Bensley was married to Emma Agnes, daughter of a wealthy aristocratic family from England. They had three daughters. Their eldest daughter Helen was married to Thomas Austin, an Indian gentleman, who worked in Bensley's bank. They had eight children. Dorothy Hope Austin, the youngest, grew up in the patrician splendour of the noble family. She completed her High School in Coonoor, Nilgiris, graduated from Madras Christian College, Madras, and moved to Bombay as a teacher at the Cathedral & John Connon School.

And now she stood there, waiting uncertainly for a stranger in a club.

Jack returned in a flash with two bottles of Coke in hand.

'One for Doe and one for Jack,' he said, handing her the bottle. 'Cheers!'

Dorothy debated whether to be offended or attracted to this audacious, handsome guy. What she did not know was that in his eyes, they were already a match.

Before Jack could request her for a dance, her brother joined them, shook hands with Jack and escorted Dorothy to the dance floor.

As she moved away, Jack whispered into her ear, 'You are a beautiful woman. When are you going to let me take you out?' Normally she would have demurred, but Dorothy just beamed at him as she floated away to the dance floor.

In that moment, Jack knew Dorothy was the one for him. He had felt an immediate, inexplicable bond with her, and of course, she was beautiful. It felt as if they had met before.

All through the next week, he tried in vain to contact her, despite his busy schedule. Then lady luck smiled at him.

Two of his mates asked Jack to join them as they were going to the Cathedral & John Connon School to pick up some lady teachers for a dance at the Gymkhana Club. John Connon School rang a bell! Dorothy! *Serendipity or cosmic energy*, Jack wondered, telling himself not to be too optimistic. He decided to go along anyway.

As they reached the school, a young lady came out to receive them. She blushed and giggled the moment she saw Jack.

'Youuuu!' she exclaimed, smiling from cheek to cheek. 'What brings you here? Nice to see you again.' Her cheeks turned crimson pink and her heart felt the first flush of a romance.

Jack gazed back adoringly at her. He couldn't believe his luck. He gathered his wits as Dorothy stretched a delicate hand towards him. 'You bring me here,' he wanted to say but was interrupted.

'Oh! You know each other,' said one of the mates.

'Of course! Of course!' mumbled Jack, taking her hand. A tingling warmth ran down his spine.

'That settles it then. Jack, you are with Dorothy as she is without a companion,' said the mate. Bemused at this unexpected stroke of luck, Jack bowed his head and thanked the Almighty for inextricably linking his life with Dorothy.

They went out to the Bombay Gymkhana Club, where over 200 guests were partaking in the joys of fine dining, live band and fine spirits.

'What will it be, Doe? Beer, whisky, brandy, Coca Cola, or would you like to dance,' asked Jack, as they entered the club.

'I would love to have a chilled Co . . .,' and Jack was gone before she completed her sentence and was back with a Coke in each hand. He handed her the Coke and began 'One for . . .,' when Dorothy put her finger on his lips, looked into his confused eyes and whispered, 'One for Jack and one for Doe. Doe for Jack and Jack for Doe. Cheers!'

'What the hell! God! How can you be so kind!' was all Jack could murmur in euphoric disbelief. Dorothy broke into uncontrolled laughter as she found Jack's innocence irresistible.

'Would you like to walk in the lawn,' said Jack, as he offered his hand and walked with her. A gentle breeze greeted them as they came out of the main hall. They walked, and talked, and talked, lost in their own world till Dorothy saw a bench and pulled Jack by his hand to make him sit next to her.

Jack moved closer to Dorothy and whispered, 'So Doe, who do you like?'

'You, you, a thousand times you,' she wanted to say. Instead, she shrugged her shoulders and looked towards her feet. Jack looked at her with a cautious smile. 'If I tell you mine, then will you tell me yours?'

'Okay,' she said.

'The one and only one I like is you!' said Jack, as he wrapped his arms around her. 'You are a beautiful woman. I can't deny my feelings for you. From the moment I met you, what I feel for you is love.'

Dorothy felt happier than she had ever felt before.

'And the one and only one I like is you,' replied Dorothy, looking into his eyes. 'I adore your charming smile, your impeccable manners, and the way you look at me.'

Jack embraced her tightly, lowered his head, and kissed her. They were locked in bliss for a long time till a gentle drizzle drenched them back to reality.

Their courtship grew warmer and more passionate with every passing day. Jack was head over heels in love with this beautiful vivacious woman, blessed with every imaginable attribute that a partner, lover, and mother could have. She would make him smile, and every time he spoke with her about his troubles, they seemed to vanish. He felt complete and content with her. This incredibly precious connection would define their future forever.

Six months after they had begun to build their beautiful bond of love, Jack was posted to Weymouth, England, to undergo a Specialisation Course for one year. Dorothy was distraught. A day before his departure, Jack asked Dorothy out for dinner.

'I brought this for you,' he said, handing her a vintage jewellery box. 'My father gave this to me ten years back. It is mine to keep, but now I entrust it to your love and care.' Inside was a hand-crafted gold ring with MSM embossed in the centre and small diamonds studded all around it. Dorothy was speechless. All her anxiety and apprehensions faded away in a flash. She held the box close to her bosom.

'Thank you, Jack. I shall cherish this forever.'

Once in England, Jack wrote her a letter every day, professing his love and the promise to marry her. Dorothy too wrote him every day about her time in school and the life she was planning for them.

Three months into the Long Course, Jack booked a trunk call to Dorothy from England and extended the proposal for marriage. Dorothy was delirious with joy. They decided that Dorothy would travel to Southampton, England, with her sister Sheila, on a forty-five-day voyage across the sea.

Dorothy's excitement grew with every sunrise as she waited impatiently to leave for England. She and Sheila spent a lot of time preparing the trousseau and selecting a beautiful wedding dress for her. She used up all her savings, including some money given by her mother for her wedding.

Jack paid for the passage for Dorothy and her sister Sheila. They were fortunate to be booked on the latest liner with state-of-the-art facilities. Their twin-bed cabin was more than comfortable. The ship had plenty to offer to make the long voyage enjoyable. Multi-cuisine menus, live band every evening, weekend dance galas, daily movies, a well-stocked library, sunbathing on the deck and, most of all, a formal six-course meal with the Captain of the ship. Dorothy and Sheila, the two prettiest young ladies on the ship, would often get preferred service.

The vessel sailed closer to its destination, winding around the Cape of Good Hope. The sea was usually calm, with choppy waves now and then. All through the journey, Dorothy missed Jack, but Sheila managed to keep her in good humour. She also listened to Dorothy's stories about the time spent with Jack.

They arrived in Southampton in early March 1951. Jack and his friend Mazhar Khan were at the docks to receive them. Jack gifted her a beautiful bouquet of 100 pink English roses. The card on the bouquet read 'Deeply love you for what you are, my joy, my life.' Dorothy was overcome with emotion. Jack held her in a tight embrace and gently kissed the tears away.

Jack and Dorothy were married on 17 March 1951, a week after she arrived in England. The wedding ceremony was conducted at the St Regis Church, Weymouth, followed by a small reception at the Navy Mess. Jack, accompanied by his best man Mazhar Khan, stood tall and handsome in his Naval uniform with the ceremonial sword. Dorothy, in her white taffeta and satin dress with pearls and diamonds as ear drops and necklace, was a vision in white. Her hair was done with a wreath of white roses and a veil of white net covered her pretty face A bouquet of white roses and green ferns adorned her hand and the train of white net fabric complemented her ethereal look. Sheila, the bridesmaid, was a picture of elegance in her pink gown.

5

Karachi Calling

I slept and dreamt that life was joy. I awoke and saw that life was service. I acted and beheld service was joy.

—*Rabindranath Tagore**

20 February 1965. Jack sat in his office in the Naval Headquarters, New Delhi, enjoying a hot cup of coffee after a gruelling day's work. Lutyens' verdant Delhi was draped in thin mist. It was well past six and most of the offices had closed for the day. Jack slid back in his chair and began to count his many blessings, as he always remembered to do.

There was, indeed, much to be grateful for. Moti Bagh, a leafy colony of officials, was a beautiful part of Delhi. Dorothy

---

* Rabindranath Tagore: From a poem in *Gitanjali*.

was a loving wife, and their four children were their treasures. The two elder boys studied at Jack's own alma mater La Martiniere College in Lucknow, a prestigious boarding school. The two younger children were day scholars in New Delhi. Thoughts of his family always brought a smile to Jack's countenance.

He was shaken from his reverie with a gentle knock on the door. He looked in the direction and saw the diminutive figure of Captain Batra, his immediate boss.

'Congratulations, Jack,' said Batra, entering the room. 'It's a double bonanza for you, my man. You have been promoted to be a Captain, and . . .' he paused for a while, expecting to see the anxiety on Jack's face. But the cool cucumber that Jack was, his expression remained nonchalant. '. . . and you have been posted as a Naval Attaché to our High Commission in Karachi.'

Instead of frowning, Jack greeted the news with a soft smile and a word of thanks.

'Great. You have two months to prepare,' Batra finished.

In his early forties, Commander Jack Shea was a top-rung officer and a skilled sailor. Most of his peers would give anything to reach the dizzy heights that he had scaled. So, Jack's promotion and selection for a prestigious foreign assignment had always been a foregone conclusion.

On reaching home, he broke the news to Dorothy. As expected, she responded with mixed feelings. While she was happy to learn about the promotion, she had some concerns about the posting to Karachi. Dorothy was expecting Jack's fifth child and a bit uncomfortable with the thought of delivering the baby in a country inimical to Indian interests.

The move to Karachi was planned for the month of May, as both the elder boys would be on summer vacation and could accompany them. There was much to be done before that, of course. The next couple of months were spent completing the innumerable formalities involving a shift of residence. The children, in their blissful innocence, excitedly shared the news with their friends and watched the house wind up with clockwork precision. And then came the day. The Shea family set sail for Karachi from Bombay aboard Sabarmati, a merchant vessel of high repute.

They arrived in Karachi and were escorted to their new residential house, Hindustan Court. Most Indian Diplomats, except the High Commissioner and Deputy High Commissioner, were housed in this gated compound, beautifully appointed with large lawns and the best amenities. There were two large bungalows in Hindustan Court, with accommodation for six families—five were already occupied by the Army Attaché, the Air Force Attaché, First Secretary Amar Singh, First Secretary Prem Dewan, Second Secretary Puri. The first floor of the larger of the two bungalows became home to the Shea family for the next two-and-a-half years.

It was a beautiful house, with a spacious living room and a grand dining room that had an attached kitchen and pantry. The bedrooms were on the other side of the house, with attached bathrooms and dressing rooms. The compound had a huge gate that was always locked. Staff accommodation was at the rear, behind the garages. A large veranda overlooked the gardens, where Jack would sit every evening and read his official papers. The children would invariably be playing outdoors until their mother called them in for dinner.

As the family settled into the new accommodation, they had to get used to living in an overtly hostile environment. It was a trying time for them, especially the younger ones, who were neither accustomed to nor could comprehend such indifference and hostility. The elder boys were a great help in getting the family to adjust to the new environment, as they kept the excitement alive through their interesting narration of whatever new they observed. The two younger children, Debora, who was in standard four, and Jon, who was in standard three, had to join a school in Karachi. Dorothy felt that it would be better for them to join a convent school run by the nuns. Jack, who generally did not interfere in Dorothy's decisions, willingly accepted the suggestion and enrolled the children in the Convent of Jesus and Mary, Clifton.

One particular memory of those days that the family would always carry was the visits to Hawkesbay Beach. Located 20 km outside of Karachi, the beautiful, sandy beach was named after Bladen Hawke, a British Conservative politician who owned a house there in the 1930s. The Indian High Commission had a shack on the beach, and all its personnel were welcome to go there and enjoy a frolic in the sea.

Jack had heard about the green turtles who came to nest over there, and he was keen to take the children to view it. Muthu, the driver, suggested that the full moon was the best time to get a glimpse of the famous turtle nesting. So, after dinner one night, Jack, Dorothy and the four children drove to Hawkesbay. There were no streetlights, but the moon was bright enough to show the way. Muthu parked near the shack, and everyone got out and ran towards the beach. Roger had to keep a sharp eye on five-year-old Jon, making sure the little one did not run into the water. The family scrambled onto scattered rocks, waiting for the turtles to emerge.

The beaches of Pakistan, namely Hawkesbay and Sandspit are among some of the most important nesting grounds for green turtles, who arrive there in thousands to lay their eggs. The nesting time is between July and December. As soon as the sun sets, the turtles, each weighing between 200 to 500 pounds come out of the ocean and pull themselves up past the high tide mark. They dig up a hole to sit in. Then with their hind flippers, they dig a cylindrical egg pit, a few feet deep. A turtle in a clutch lays up to about 100 to 150 eggs into the pit. Afterwards, she covers both the hole and the pit with sand and then pulls herself back into the sea.

About eight weeks after the eggs are laid, on a full moon night, you can witness the spectacle of thousands of tiny turtles crawling towards the ocean.

The moon lit up the beach, and the waves splashing against the sand. The weather was warm and pleasant, and a gentle breeze whistled. They had been waiting for nearly an hour when Ian yelled, 'Hey! I can see them. They are like an army!'

They rushed down to the sandy beach to see thousands of tiny turtles emerging from their nesting pits and crawling their way towards the sea. The entire beach had transformed into a carpet of moving green.

It was such a fantastic sight; once seen, never forgotten. The unimaginable visual of the splendour of nature. They sat there, mesmerised. Crawling out of the pit, the hatchlings dusted the sand off themselves for a few moments and then trudged along like soldiers towards the ocean.

It was late, and the breeze was getting a little chilly. Jack and Dorothy led the children towards the car. They scrambled in and drove back. It was an amazing story to tell their friends when they got back to their school.

Time flew. The elder boys began packing to return to school in India. They would fly from Karachi to New Delhi, where they would be met by a liaison person from the Indian Navy and escorted to the railway station. From there, a reserved coach would take them to their school.

As the family bid farewell to the boys at the Karachi International Airport, they took a family photograph, a rarity in those times.

6

Harassed and Embarrassed

Every once in a while, the Pakistani top brass would flex some muscle, reiterating their presence in the diplomatic circles. One such event had the Pakistani President, General Ayub Khan taking a turn on the red carpet. It was a splendid State Banquet arranged at the Presidential Palace. The guest list covered the entire spectrum of Embassies, and all the incumbent diplomats and their wives. There was fine wine and Scotch whiskey. Dinner was a seven-course meal of caviar, salmon, lobster and the choicest cuisine.

It was impressive to say the least. The Indian chapter were feeling chuffed in their corner.

The telephone rang out, and Jack's secretary answered.

'May I speak to Captain Shea?' came a crisp voice.

'Who may I say is calling?'

'This is a call from the Ministry of Interior.'

'Certainly, Sir. Just one moment. Allow me to check his availability.'

She buzzed Jack on his intercom.

'Yes.'

'Sir, there is somebody on the line from the Ministry of Interior. He'd like to speak with you.'

'Yes, of course, please put him through.'

She disconnected the Intercom and connected Jack onto the line.

'Good morning, Sir. I have received a memo from the Ministry of Interior. I can come over to your office and hand it over to you. It is of a sensitive nature,' said the caller.

'Good morning. I will be in the office the entire day. You may come at your convenience. Please give your name and designation to my secretary and she will arrange your entry pass at the Security gate. Thank you. Have a good day,' said Jack.

A few hours later, Major Rasool Rizwan was ushered into Jack Shea's office.

'Good afternoon, Sir!'

Jack wished him and indicated towards a chair.

'Sir, a few days back, there was a State Banquet held at the Presidential Palace. You and your wife had attended the banquet. Some guests have made an observation that your wife remained seated while the Pakistani National Anthem was being played.'

Jack was taken aback. He stared at the Major, trying to process what the man had just said.

'I'm not able to understand what it is that you are implying.'

'Sir, your wife remained seated during the rendition of the Pakistani National Anthem. Under our law, this is an act of sedition. Your wife must accompany us to the Ministry for questioning.'

'I'm sorry, my friend, but my wife cannot accompany you. She is in the family way. And her health is fragile. It is preposterous for you to presume that she remained seated during the Pakistani National Anthem. She has been a Defence Forces wife for many years, and she is well versed in State level protocol.'

'I'm sorry, Sir, but a written complaint has been filed and we must address the matter.'

'How are you sure it was my wife? We have just arrived in Pakistan and I'm sure not too many people know her.'

'Sir, she was recognized by Captain Mazhar Khan. He was seated at the same table as Mrs Shea. I believe he is well acquainted with yourself and Mrs Shea.'

This was a double whammy. Mazhar Khan had been the best man at Jack and Dorothy's wedding in Weymouth, where Jack and Mazhar had done the Long Course together. They had gone to the opposite sides of the border when India and Pakistan were partitioned. But they had always been good friends. Or that was what Jack had thought. This was such an unpalatable revelation; an 'Et tu, Brute?' moment.

Jack took a few moments to regain his composure.

Finally, he said, 'Oh, well, in that case, I will have to run this past the High Commissioner. Kindly leave your name and contact number with my secretary, and I will get back to you. Please leave the memo with me.'

Major Rasool Rizwan handed the envelope with the written memo inside it to Jack. He was silently impressed with the Captain's composure. He took his leave and left the office, escorted to the door by Jack's Secretary.

Soon enough, Jack buzzed the High Commissioner on the Intercom.

'Sir, are you free for a couple of minutes? I need to discuss something of a sensitive nature with you.'

'Yes Jack, you can come over. I'm free as of now.'

Jack felt his core tighten as he stepped out of his office. They were attacking his Achilles heel; his beloved wife Dorothy—his anchor in every storm. Carrying the memo, he climbed up a flight of steps to the High Commissioner's office, knocked on the door and entered.

'Good morning, Jack! What brings you here, bright and early?'

'I had a visitor this morning from the Pakistan Interior Ministry. He handed over a memo to me, alleging that Dorothy was seated when the Pakistan National Anthem was being played, at the State Banquet held a few days ago. President Ayub Khan was in attendance at the Presidential Palace.'

The gentle smile faded on the High Commissioner's face.

'This is preposterous! The lengths these people will go to embarrass and harass Indian Diplomats.'

The High Commissioner decided to buzz the Deputy High Commissioner, Uma Shankar Bajpai, on the Intercom.

'Uma, do you have a minute?'

'Yes, Sir.'

'Please step into my office. I'd like to have a word with you.'

'Sure. Coming up.'

The Deputy High Commissioner was a refined gentleman with impeccable manners and a steely resolve, concealed under a smooth, suave demeanour. Never one to mince his words, always conveyed in silken tones.

He stepped into the High Commissioner's office and saw Jack seated at the desk. Jack rose from his chair and greeted Uma.

'We had a visitor from the Interior Ministry today. He had a memo for Jack. Apparently, there's an observation that during the State Banquet hosted by President Ayub Khan, held a few days back, Dorothy remained seated during the Pakistan National Anthem. And they are asking us to bring her to the Ministry for questioning.'

'This is ridiculous!' exclaimed Uma.

He thought for a while. 'We will have to counter this officially. How best can we do this?'

The three of them remained silent for a few minutes, weighing all the options available to them. One thing was for sure; they would not allow them to target the families and the ladies. It was hitting below the belt.

After a while, Uma said, 'Dorothy was seated at my table, and I can give a statement that I saw she was standing when they played the National Anthem. I can be a witness. I'm sure that should suffice.'

High Commissioner G. Parthasarathy was relieved to hear Uma's words.

'You and Jack can go over to the Ministry tomorrow and give them a written statement.'

'Yes sure. We can do that. Let me know where and what time; we can go together Jack.'

'Yes, Sir. I'll take an appointment with the Secretary for the Interior Ministry.'

'Ok, that's done then. Let us get back to work.'

The three of them shook hands and left the office.

At the end of the day, Muthu drove Jack back home. Jack was keyed up and pensive. It hurt him to think that they were targeting his wife and family. Their little daughter was still recovering from a nasty fall from the window. And now this. Dorothy was expecting and much too fragile to enter any Ministry for questioning. It kept playing on his mind, and he was unusually subdued during dinner. But he dared not mention it to Dorothy, knowing it would distress her immensely.

The next day, Jack's Secretary made an appointment with the concerned official in the Ministry of Interior. Both Uma and Jack left for the Ministry in Uma's car.

At the reception, they were ushered into the concerned person's office after they identified themselves.

Uma came to the point directly without wasting time on etiquette. 'We are here to respond to a memo, which one of your people came and delivered to Captain Shea yesterday. At the outset, let me state categorically that Mrs Dorothy was seated at my table. And I observed that she was standing when the Pakistan National Anthem was being played. I will give you a written statement to this effect. Please also be advised that I shall take this matter up with our Ministry of External Affairs. There appears to be a concerted effort to make false allegations and target the families of Indian Diplomats in Pakistan. Thereafter you may be required to respond to that.'

The tone that Uma used was terse but exceedingly polite. He and Jack saw the officer go red in the face. He stuttered apologetically. 'We are only carrying out an enquiry on some allegation made by a senior Defence personnel.'

'Sir, I am sure that you are aware that the lady is not well, and in the family way. This is an attack on our sensitivities. I would greatly appreciate it if you did not indulge in such activities in the future.'

'Sir, I was not aware the lady was indisposed. I apologise if there has been any transgression.'

'It will not reflect well on the Government, should this episode be reported to our Ministry.'

'Allow me to urge you to re-think on this matter. We shall accept your written statement and close the matter here immediately.'

'That will be all, Sir. I take your leave.'

Uma and Jack got up shook hands with the Pakistani officer and left the building.

While they were driving back, Uma burst out, 'Scoundrels! They can sink to any depths to embarrass and harass us. But don't worry, they won't trouble Dorothy now. We always have to hit back harder when they attack us, and they will retreat into a corner. I shall send off a letter citing this episode to the MEA. Thereafter, the Ministry will take over. Well, well, so ends another day at the office!' He patted Jack's hand briefly.

They drove quietly towards the High Commission. Another battle had been fought and won.

7

House Arrest

*No one who does good work will ever come to a bad end, either
here or in the world to come.*

—*The Bhagavad Gita**

India was still smarting from the humiliating defeat in the
1962 Indo-China War. The country had been ill-prepared for a
conflict with its northern neighbour. The political dispensation
of the day had assumed that signing the Panchsheel Agreement
with China would solve the issues between the two great
neighbours. Thus, no strategy or preparation was in place to
tackle any threat from China, despite their occupation of Tibet
in 1950 and overthrow of the Tibetan Government in 1959.

---

* The Bhagwad Gita.

The humiliating defeat at the hands of the Chinese dealt a severe blow to the morale of the Indian Army, which took some time to recover.

Relations with Pakistan were deteriorating, too. The Mission staff now required more surveillance and increased reconnaissance. The mantle for gathering information about Naval assets and their deployment fell on Jack, who accepted it with alacrity. While diplomatic outreach helped in fact-finding, the ground situation and the level of preparedness of the Pakistan Navy could only be ascertained by visiting the Karachi Harbour.

Taking advantage of his location and status, Jack made several visits to military areas that were not accessible to civilians. However, he knew that gathering any information from the harbour would have to be done surreptitiously. Though not trained in espionage, Jack kept himself informed about the activities of agencies like the CIA, KGB, and Mossad. It didn't take him much time to formulate a clear plan to get close to the Naval assets, without being tracked.

Jack hired a boat and took his children fishing one weekend. He started from the jetty close to a fishing village. The children carried one fishing rod with a bait hanging to it and Jack carried another. The sea was usually calm, so Jack asked the boatman to stop the boat way out from the harbour. Undisturbed waters ensured that they would get a good catch, and after a while, Jack asked the boatman to change the location and guide him to steer the boat in the direction of the harbour. Soon, they were heading towards the Naval Jetty where some warships were anchored alongside each other. The boatman slowed down, as a matter of abundant caution, as he drew close to the Naval area.

The children, delighted to see their father pull out a camera, posed willingly for photographs. Unobtrusively, Jack lay down at the bottom of the boat and photographed the warships. To keep the boatman in good humour and willing to take them on the next trip, Jack shared the catch with him.

Two fishing trips, spaced a fortnight apart, were enough to gather the information Jack sought.

Late in the evening of 18 August, Dorothy went into labour. Jack took her to the Seventh Day Adventist Hospital in Karachi. It was a tricky delivery as the baby was lodged in the birth canal in an awkward position and his heartbeat had started to get feeble. Dr. Maria D'Souza had to forcibly extricate the baby. Unfortunately, the procedure caused the infant's right elbow to be fractured. He also swallowed a lot of the amniotic fluid, causing congestion of the lungs. He was put into an incubator and a team of doctors worked on him all night to clear his lungs. His arm was put into a cast, and the little fellow was ready to go home in a few days.

Border skirmishes that began between the two countries in April 1965 came to a head in August that year. Although Kashmir was the predominant issue, other border disputes existed, most notably over the Rann of Kutch, a barren region in the Indian state of Gujarat. Pakistan, under the leadership of General Ayub Khan, was desperate to complete their unfinished post-Partition agenda to take over the entire state of Jammu and Kashmir. They somehow believed that the Indian Army, weakened from its heavy loss to China, would be unable to defend itself against a quick military campaign. The General, convinced that the population of Kashmir was largely discontent with Indian rule, started covert infiltration of saboteurs, code-named 'Operation Gibraltar,' to ignite a resistance movement amongst the locals.

On 5 August 1965, over 30,000 Pakistani soldiers, dressed as Kashmiri locals, crossed the Line of Control and headed for various areas within Kashmir. Indian forces, well prepared for such an eventuality, offered stiff resistance, causing heavy casualties to the intruders. Both Armies engaged in a pitched artillery battle, mostly on the border areas of Jammu and Kashmir and the Rann of Kutch.

All through this, life in the enclosed and secure Hindustan Court, an island of decency and harmony, remained comfortable and peaceful. However, unabated propaganda on the radio and in the newspapers about the elusive victories of the Pakistan Army over Indian troops was a matter of discomfort and concern to the residents.

A few days before the open declaration of war, three Pakistani military trucks entered Hindustan Court, loaded with approximately sixty soldiers and a lot of equipment. They formed two groups and started assembling tents on the lawns. Two large and two small tents were erected. The large tents were set up to accommodate the troops and the small ones to function as a kitchen and a toilet. Once the tents were up, their senior officer asked all the residents of Hindustan Court to assemble in the courtyard.

All members of the six families residing in Hindustan Court came down, except the toddlers. This was perhaps the first time that members of the diplomatic corps and their families had been subjected to military regimen. The officer spoke in chaste Urdu laden with a heavy Punjabi accent. Jack and his anglicised family struggled to get the drift of his expostulations. Of course, it was much worse for Prem Dewan and his family, who were Tamilians and did not know a word of Hindi, much less Urdu.

The Pakistani officer, a Major in the army, rattled off the 'model code of conduct' to be followed by all residents. His rude tone and tenor indicated that he meant business. No one was allowed to go out of Hindustan Court, no visits to the market. Servants were not allowed inside the compound. All telephones were disconnected. Further, every household would host one more Indian family. In essence, it was a house arrest.

A day later, George Truter, Second Secretary at the Indian High Commission, along with his wife Ita and son Barry, came to live in the Shea house. The children were excited to have another companion. Dorothy was still busy with post-natal check-ups and follow-ups on her newborn's lungs and arm. Sulaiman, the cook from Kanpur, had accompanied the family to Karachi and was a real pillar of strength to Dorothy in these uncertain times, as despite restrictions and dwindling supplies he would churn out delicious meals for all.

All window panels in the houses were covered with black paper, and bulbs were removed to ensure total blackout. Playing the radio was not permitted. Television was in a nascent stage in Pakistan and telecast only local programs, spewing propaganda and rhetoric that were of no interest to the Indian families, so hardly anyone had procured a TV set. The soldiers would frequently come into the house to search. On one occasion, they confiscated two personal weapons belonging to Jack, a pistol and a revolver.

One day in the last week of August, after the High Commissioner's briefing on the inevitable war with Pakistan, all diplomats were busy working till late in the evening. They called it a day at 7.00 p.m. and moved to return home. As they arrived, they were appalled to see that a large number of Pakistani policemen and soldiers had barricaded the gate, prohibiting any entry or exit. On a query from the officer in charge of the troops, it was revealed that the High Commission and its occupants were under threat of an attack from angry mobs who had assembled in thousands as they were extremely angry at the unjust war being waged by India against Pakistan. So, the barricading and deployment of troops was to protect the High Commission and its occupants. They were detained at the High Commission Office for three days under the pretext that it was unsafe to leave the High Commission till further instructions from the Ministry of Home Affairs of Pakistan.

Soon the available supply of food articles ran out in all houses in Hindustan Court. There was no food to cook, and the soldiers would not allow the staff to go to the stores to buy food supplies. They were to prepare whatever was in the house. Dorothy had stored some tinned food for a rainy day, which came in handy then. Children, who were often seen with a can of Coca-Cola or Pepsi, now played around empty-handed. The situation seemed to be spiraling out of control with every passing day and was exacerbated by the intimidating presence of the soldiers and the absence of the man of the house.

To make matters worse, the plaster cast around the newborn baby's arm was tightening, as he was gaining weight. It caused him extreme discomfort and he would cry a lot, at times through the night, waking up everyone. Soon the arm started turning blue due to inadequate blood supply, leaving Dorothy beside herself with anxiety. She didn't know what to do, where to go or whom to turn to. Jack was not there and could not be spoken to, as the soldiers would not allow her to use the telephone in their temporary office.

In sheer desperation, she approached the Major. After a lot of persuasion, he permitted her to make a call to the doctor.

She explained the condition of the baby's arm to Dr. D'Souza, who asked her to rush him to the hospital. Despite repeated pleas from Dorothy and the doctor, the Major wouldn't allow Dorothy to leave the place.

Left with no other option, the doctor, herself a mother of three children, decided to carry some rudimentary equipment and drove to Hindustan Court. The gate was manned by soldiers, who refused to let her enter. Dorothy, with her screaming baby in her arms, rushed to the gate and pleaded with them, but they did not allow either the doctor to come in or Dorothy to go out. Eventually, as the baby's screams got shriller, the Major asked Dorothy to hand over the infant through the gate to the doctor. Though appalled at such inhuman behavior, she had no choice. With much trepidation, she handed over the baby to Doctor D'Souza.

The doctor immediately administered a pain reliever to the baby via a dropper. Her assistant then prepared a small area on the rear seat of the vehicle and laid the baby there. With utmost caution, the doctor began cutting away small bits of the plaster with a sharp blade. At last, the plaster came off, and she gave a gentle massage to the arm to restore circulation. The poor little one's misery was relieved immediately. He stopped crying and let out a gentle smile.

She lifted the baby gently, applied a soothing gel to his arm, and bandaged it in soft crepe bandage, which could be removed and redone in case it got too tight.

She handed back the baby to Dorothy. Dorothy hugged her little boy, tears streaming down her cheeks, and thanked the doctor. She walked back to the house, sobbing all the way up the steps to her house. She went to the balcony and sat there with the baby in her arms. Her two younger children Debora and Jon stood helplessly next to her. They would realize much later that those trying times were bringing them closer than ever. And that the bond thus forged would last throughout their lives.

8

Hunger & Anger inside Hindustan Court

There is no avoiding war; it can only be postponed to the advantage of others.

—*Niccolo Machiavelli**

Jack returned home after three days of forced confinement at the High Commission, only to see Dorothy in a very fragile state. He took her in his arms, and she sobbed into his shoulder. The children too rallied around their father and clung to him. All four remained in a tight embrace for a long time and then slowly moved together to the parents' bedroom.

Jack gazed lovingly at his ten-day-old baby, fast asleep in his crib. There was no evidence that he had just been through

---

* Niccolo Machiavelli: From his book *The Prince*.

two days of harrowing pain. It was such a relief for the family to have Jack around again. His mere presence was a reassurance to them. It felt as if now all would be well.

Pakistani soldiers deployed in Hindustan Court would patrol around the houses after 7.00 p.m. and yell at everyone to switch off the lights. The residents, helpless under the circumstances, would sit huddled together in total darkness. The only source of light was the candles, used one at a time during dinner. Air-raid warning sirens would go off frequently, and airplanes could be heard passing over the houses, triggering fear of impending aerial bombing.

But Jack, despite the uncertain times and paucity of food, maintained his poise. He would go for walks in the evening with his children. Other residents, including the ladies, would also take a stroll. They would all congregate at some point and chat to keep each other's spirits high. They walked around till sunset and broke up when the soldiers gestured at them to go back into their houses.

The uncertain nights were composed of a modest meal, unhappy thoughts, and restless sleep. Debora and Jon, both very young, shared almost everything. They slept in the same room, woke up together, had their meals together, went to school together, and played together.

During the war, they were too scared to sleep in their own room and slept in their parents' bedroom, tucked between mom and dad. The new-born had his own crib at the foot of the bed.

Shortage of food soon became a major issue as none of the six families had any reserves. No one had been prepared for the eventuality of war or house arrest, so there were no contingent reserves. Each household had to support another family of three to four members. By the sixth day, the Sheas had to make do with rice and *kanji*. (The water in which rice is boiled is called kanji in South India.)

While the men knew they had no choice but to maintain the status quo, some of the ladies thought it apt to approach the Pakistani Major and request him to arrange for some food supplies. The Major frostily declined to be of any help, stating it was beyond his brief. The ladies returned home despondent, only to return to the Major when the sight of their empty pantries and hungry children greeted them.

It was around 8.00 p.m. The Pakistani Major was sitting outside his tent on the lawn, chewing paan after enjoying a sumptuous meal prepared by the Company cook. Seeing the small group of ladies approaching him, he stood up to go inside his tent. He was in no mood to entertain some shrieking women. One of the ladies stepped forward and blocked his way. This was Brigadier Kamran's wife Promila, a 5-feet 8-inch strapping Sardarni. The Major, taken aback by the lady's temerity, glared.

'Major Saab, *khaana ho gaya?*' (Have you had your dinner, Major?) she asked. He nodded. By now, the others in the group of eight had surrounded him.

'I'm glad you have eaten, Major Saab, because we haven't,' said Promila.

'Oh, oh! Why is that?' He inquired, feigning innocence.

'There's nothing to eat in our houses and our children are starving. How can you be so inhuman and enjoy a feast while they sleep hungry?'

'But I have my orders, I cannot break my orders. There's nothing I can do,' the Major blurted. 'We have cooked some food here for our men, I can send it to your houses,' he added, a bit intimidated by the indignant looks that were pointed his way.

Though the offer was condescending and humiliating, the ladies had no choice but to accept. Within a short while, the soldiers brought around food containers to each household. The food, typical army battalion standard, was spicy but delicious. The residents were happy to have a decent meal after three days.

The absence of lights left no choice for the residents, but to go to bed early. Dawn would bring yet another uncertain day, with nothing to do but walk and exercise. A frugal breakfast of oats or barley porridge would be put together. There were no fruits, eggs, bread or butter. Their host country, Pakistan, was at war with their home country, India, which made it all the more necessary to maintain calm and harmony.

Livid at the deteriorating situation, the ladies, accompanied by their husbands, went to meet the Major again. This time, he was sitting at the entrance of his tent, and a barber was giving him a shave. He was visibly embarrassed to be caught half attired. Promila, the most vociferous of the group, spoke first, repeating what she had said the previous day, exhorting the Major to make arrangements for food articles. Taking food from their Cook House was at best a stopgap arrangement, she pointed out.

Unruffled, the Major said, 'I am just following my orders. Until I am given instructions, I am not in a position to make any changes.' That did it. Promila exploded like a volcano, unleashing the choicest expletives in Punjabi at the hapless Major, who almost fell off his chair. She was unstoppable by now. 'I will report you to the High Commissioner. What if any of us falls sick or dies while you heartlessly discharge your duties? It will be reported to our Defence Minister and similar treatment will be meted out to the people in your High Commission in New Delhi. And mind you, the UN will also take stringent diplomatic action against you for this inhuman behaviour.'

The severity of Promila's diatribe finally struck a chord. The Major stood up, wiped the shaving cream off his face, and moved away from her. He thought it was better to speak to the men, as they would be more reasonable. He spoke with Brigadier Kamran, Jack and Prem Dewan and assured them that he would speak to his seniors and take due approvals. Till then, the residents would have to abide by the rules and strictures imposed under the code of conduct.

The men agreed to adhere to his advice, but the ladies were not so cooperative. They decided to sit outside the Major's tent in a peaceful protest, till he agreed to make some arrangements to procure food. After a while, the soldiers came around and persuaded them to go back to their houses.

It was a little after 5.00 p.m. A man with a cart full of vegetables ambled along in front of the gate. A sentry on duty at the gate called out to him, '*Oye, idhar aa*' (Hey, come here). The cart-man was somewhat surprised because nobody from that compound had ever called out to him. Everybody knew the Indians (the enemy) lived there. However, business is business.

End of the day, if he was to make some money out of it, so be it. He wheeled his cart over to the gate.

'*Kya hai bhaiya?*' (What do you want, brother?) He asked the sentry.

The sentry signalled to him to wait as the residents of the compound wanted to buy some vegetables. Very quickly, word got around, and within a flash, the cooks and the ladies of the houses rushed to the gate. Before the cart-man could figure out what had hit him, the cart was empty and his hands were full of cash. So what if the money was from the enemy camp, he thought gleefully, 'All is fair in love and war!'

Pushing his luck along with his empty cart, he ventured, '*Kal phir se aaon?*' (Shall I come again tomorrow?)

The sentry grunted, '*Haan haan, aa jana*' (Yes, you can come).

The kitchens in the complex suddenly came alive. The sound of chopping and the smell of frying filled the air again. That morning, the adage 'Good food makes happy people' applied most fittingly to the people of Hindustan Court.

The attempt by Pakistan to seize Jammu and Kashmir proved futile. India used its potent air power and gallant ground forces along the entire Western front and checkmated Pakistan at every step. The war reached a stalemate. India moved quickly to internationalise the regional dispute, asking the United Nations to end the conflict. The Security Council passed Resolution 211 on 20 September, calling for an end to the fighting and negotiations on the settlement of the Kashmir problem. India and Pakistan declared a ceasefire on 22 September 1965.

That alone did not resolve the status of Kashmir, and both sides accepted the Soviet Union as a third-party mediator. Negotiations in Tashkent between Prime Minister Lal Bahadur Shastri of India and President Ayub Khan of Pakistan concluded on 10 January 1966. The agreement was mediated by Soviet Premier Alexei Kosygin, who had invited the parties to Tashkent. Both parties agreed to withdraw all armed forces to positions held before 5 August 1965—to restore diplomatic relations and to discuss economic, refugee, and other questions.

The Indian Prime Minister had serious reservations about certain aspects of the Tashkent Agreement, as it did not contain a no-war pact or any renunciation of guerrilla aggression in Kashmir. But Kosygin was able to persuade him to agree to sign the accord in the interest of greater peace for all.

The very next day, on 11 January 1966, India awoke to the news that Prime Minister Lal Bahadur Shastri had suffered a massive heart attack and passed away in Tashkent. His sudden demise left the Indian political system in disarray. Though diminutive in physical stature, Shastri was a towering figure in the Indian National Congress. With him, the stalwarts of the grand old Congress Party were all but gone.

The party had to rally around and elect a new Prime Minister. But there was no leader with a pan-India stature who commanded unanimous support of the party. The demise of an upright politician, who galvanised the country towards nationhood with his slogan 'Jai Jawan, Jai Kissan,' at a critical moment was the inflection point in Indian politics. A short-lived era of men of great learning, impeccable character, absolute integrity, including intellectual rectitude and great vision, who orchestrated India's independence and curated the Republic.

Deputy Prime Minister Gulzari Lal Nanda took over as the interim Prime Minister. The fragile political scenario at home affected the Indian High Commission in Pakistan for some time to come. There could be no political or military support at this juncture as India was in a stage of transition between the death of one Prime Minister and the appointment of a new one. No policy decisions and proactive action could be taken. Everything in India went into a 'status quo' freeze.

The ceasefire became effective, the soldiers of the Pakistan Army lodged in Hindustan Court vacated the premises. Telephones were reactivated but as they were sure to be tapped, the residents scarcely used them. Whilst the troops vacated the compound, vigil by the ISI increased enormously. Three men were positioned on a wall about 100 metres from the compound gate. Every time a vehicle left Hindustan Court, they would leap off the wall, jump into their waiting Volkswagen Beetle car and follow. For some unknown reason, Jack's movements were of particular interest to them—whenever he left the compound, he was followed from a safe distance.

Families sharing residences returned to their houses, and life returned to a semblance of normalcy in Hindustan Court. Diplomats returned to work at the High Commission as usual, but children were not yet allowed to go to school.

9

The Great Escape—Part 1

Prem Dewan Flees Pakistan

Stand up for something, even if it means standing alone. Because often times, one who flies solo has the strongest wings.

—*Anon**

Prem Dewan, a First Secretary in the High Commission, was actually from the Indian Police Service. He was deputed to Pakistan before the 1965 war and masterminded several surveillance ventures. He would collate information from undercover agents and transmit it to the government sources in New Delhi. His unassuming persona gave him a veneer of

---

* Anonymous.

Jack with his cousins
Olga, Maurice,
Melville and Sylvia
1927, Agra

St Regis Church,
Weymouth, England
17 March, 1951

Grandfather George Carmen, Postmaster General. 1924, Agra

Lieutenant Garnet Milton Shea aka Jack Shea. 1946, Bombay

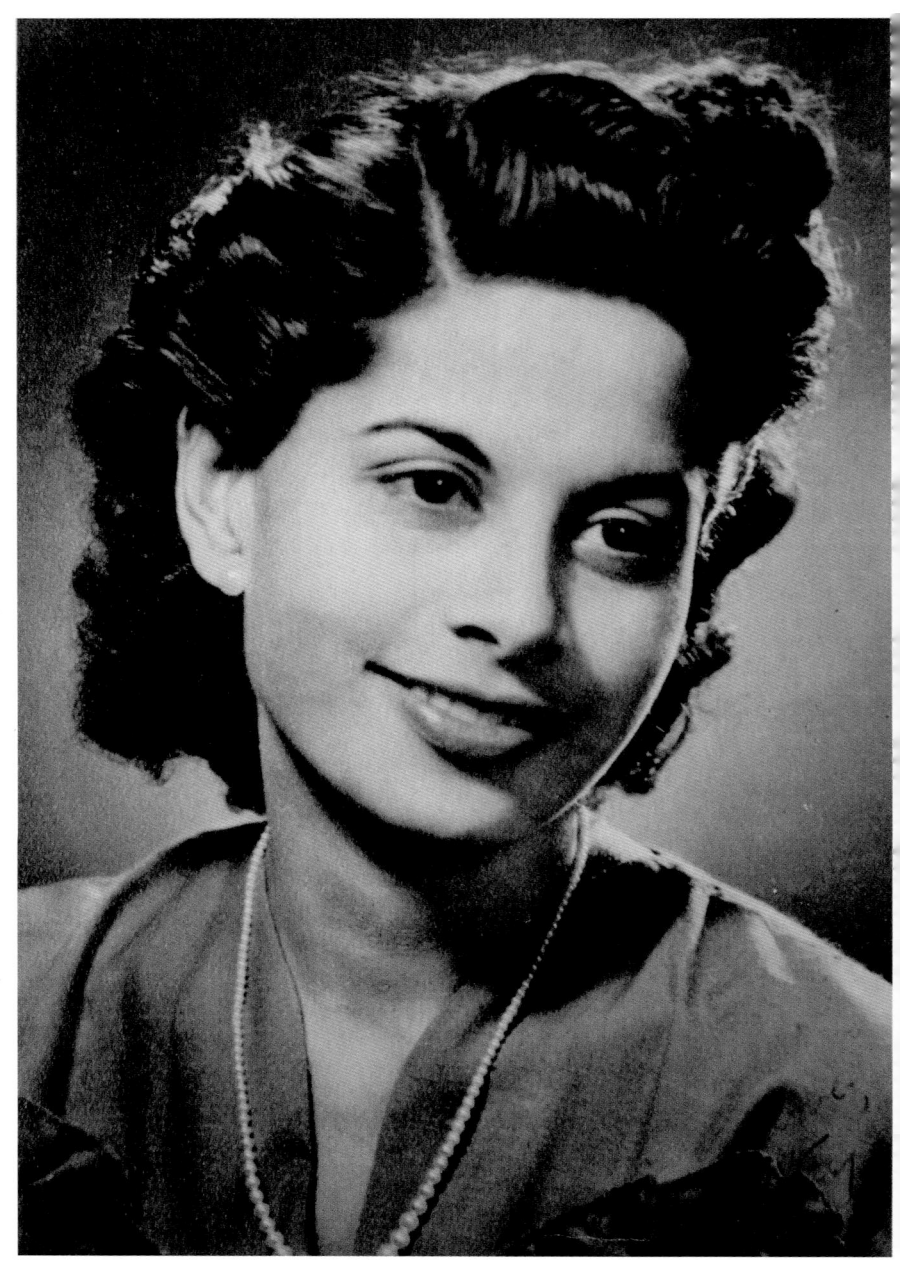

Dorothy Hope, Cathedral School. 1950, Bombay

Tactical School. 1955, Cochin

Group Captain Barua, Captain Jack Shea, Brigadier Kamran
Military Attaches to the Indian High Commission. 1965, Karachi

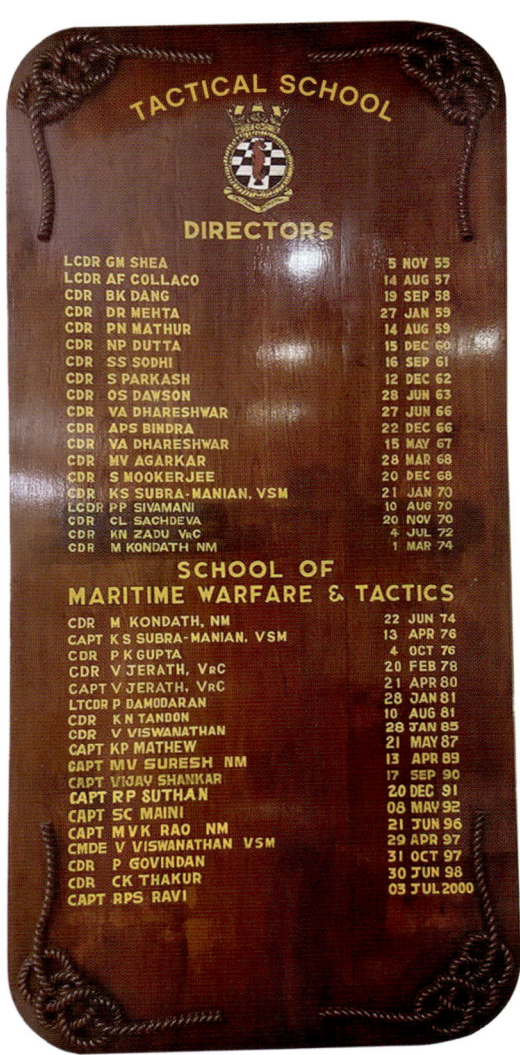

Board of Directors, Tactical School. 1955, Cochin

COMMENDATION

BY

THE CHIEF OF THE NAVAL STAFF

 I have seen your reports on important events in Pakistan, especially those concerning the Navy and the Air Force. Their contents have been very useful and the manner of presentation creditable.

 I wish to express my appreciation of your sustained efforts and initiative in the performance of your duties in very difficult circumstances.

 I have directed that a copy of this commendation be placed in your record of service.

VICE ADMIRAL
CHIEF OF THE NAVAL STAFF,
20ᵗ May 1967.

Captain Garnet Milton Shea, Indian Navy,
Naval Adviser,
Indian High Commission,
KARACHI (PAKISTAN).

Commendation letter from the Chief of Naval Staff. 1968

Jack & Dorothy
Weekend with the family
1965, Hawkesbay, Karachi

1965, Karachi.
Dorothy with the children:
Roger, Ian, Debbie & Jon

President Zakir Hussain
Ati Vishisht Seva Medal
Captain Jack Shea. 1969,
Investiture at Durbar Hall,
Rashtrapati Bhavan,
New Delhi

In Gulmarg, with the family
1964, Kashmir

Investiture Ceremony

(DEFENCE)

Rashtrapati Bhavan,
New Delhi.

16th April 1969
26 Chaitra 1891 (Saka)

ATI VISHISHT SEVA MEDAL

Captain GARNET MILTON SHEA, Indian Navy.

Captain Garnet Milton Shea joined the Indian Naval Volunteer Reserve as a Midshipman in 1943 and was commissioned as Acting Sub-Lieutenant in 1944. He saw active service in Burma during World War II. He was absorbed in the permanent cadre of the Indian Navy in 1951. In 1952 the officer was selected to undergo a specialization course in Torpedo and anti submarine in the United Kingdom. After completion of Tactical Course in the U.K. in 1955, he took over as Officer-in-Charge of the Tactical School at Cochin. When it was decided to acquire an Action Speed Tactical Teacher for the Indian Navy, Lieutenant Commander Shea was deputed to the U.K. to Study its set up and was entrusted with its installation in India. He completed the installation of the equipment in record time and thereby made a notable contribution to the future tactical training of the Indian Navy. After completing a course at the Defence Services Staff College in 1960, he was placed in command of INS KHUKRI. Thereafter, he was appointed as Deputy Director of Personnel Services (Officers) at Naval Headquarters. In 1967, he took over as Commanding Officer INS RAJPUT and Captain (D) of a Destroyer Squadron. He displayed leadership, courage and tenacity in the Salvage operation of INS SUKANYA which had run aground off the East Coast, which was commended by the Chief of the Naval Staff.

Investiture ceremony. Citation for the Ati Vishisht Seva Medal.
Captain Jack Shea

Second Ati Vishisht Seva Medal. President V V Giri
1971, Rashtrapati Bhavan, Durbar Hall

Tea with President V V Giri. Captain Jack Shea, Dorothy & Debora
1971, Rashtrapati Bhavan

Commodore Jack & Mrs. Dorothy Shea, 1971

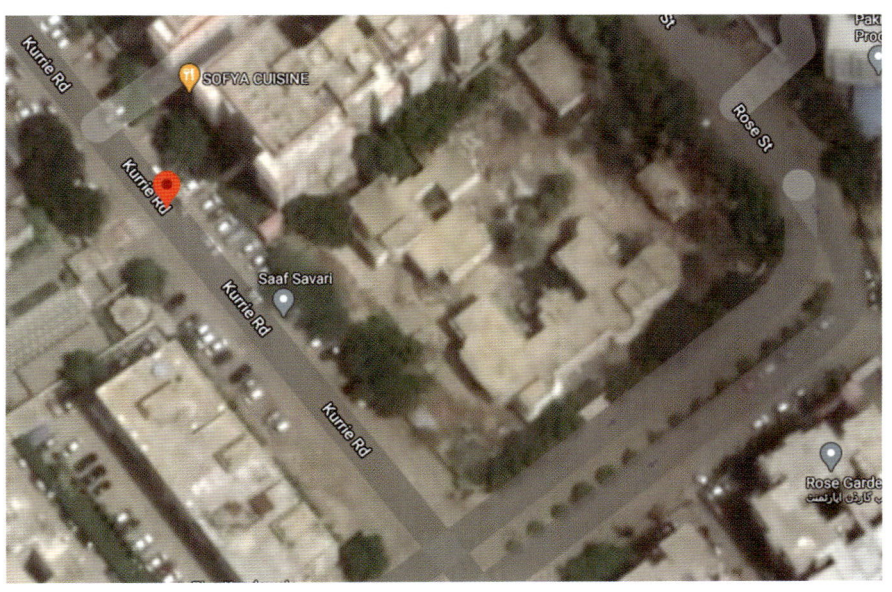

Prime Minister Mrs. Indira Gandhi, with Mrs. Dorothy Shea & Debora
1971, Rashtrapati Bhavan

Hindustan Court, Karachi, Pakistan. The compound where the Shea family resided

Captain "D", 11th Destroyer Squadron. 1969, Bombay

Defence Secretary V Shankar. C in C Western Naval Command
Admiral Kohli, Captain Jack Shea. 1969

C in C, Western Naval Command. Admiral Kohli
Captain "D." Jack Shea. 1969, INS RAJPUT

Jack Shea at his 80th birthday celebration, with all his children: Ian, Christopher,
Debora, Jonathan & Roger. 2004, The Leela, Bangalore

Commodore Jack Shea, Mrs. Jennifer Nandi,
Mrs. Dorothy Shea, Captain Fraser, Mrs. Mavis Vats,
Commander J N Vats. 1973, INS NILGIRI

innocence, saving him from suspicion. He proved to be a great asset during the war as the information passed by him kept the Indian forces a step ahead of Pakistan.

Soon, the ISI had gathered enough information to establish the presence of an undercover agent working in the Indian High Commission. Embarrassed and infuriated, the Pakistani Generals moved heaven and earth to uncover the mole who had penetrated their military ranks and attained classified information. After massive surveillance and relentless tracking, they identified their man—Prem Dewan.

Prem Dewan was an Indian diplomat, no less. As soon as New Delhi learnt of Pakistan's plans to take him into custody, High Commissioner G. Parthasarathy was instructed to secure Dewan and deport him to India most expeditiously. The High Commissioner called all three military Attaches, Deputy High Commissioner Uma Bajpai and First Secretary Prem Dewan for a meeting.

The members were of the unanimous opinion that Pakistan would take a very serious view of the espionage and the most stringent action against the spy. The conclusion was simple— Prem had to be moved out of Pakistan post-haste.

The question was, who could be trusted with the responsibility of safely extraditing Prem out of Pakistan? The room wore pin-drop silence; everyone knew how dangerous the task was going to be. They were on enemy land, and anything going wrong could be fatal. Worse, there was every chance that things could go wrong. After all, Prem was now a marked man. No doubt he would be put under 'round-the-clock' surveillance.

After a deafening silence, with no one volunteering to take on the task, Parthasarathy dismissed the meeting and asked the Deputy High Commissioner, Uma Bajpai, to stay back. He cautioned Prem to stay within the four walls of the High Commission until further instructions.

The High Commissioner and his Deputy conferred for long and settled upon a name. Jack Shea.

Late in the evening, as the diplomats were winding up for the day, Bajpai asked Jack to meet them at the office. The High Commissioner looked Jack square in the eye and asked, 'Can you handle this?' Though a little unprepared for the upfront question, Jack returned the High Commissioner's steady gaze and said with utmost confidence 'Yes Sir.'

'Good. You will have all the resources of the Indian High Commission at your disposal. You need to report only to me and no one else. And speak to me in person. Use your discretion and use it wisely.'

'Sir, I shall draw up a plan and work on its execution along with Mr. Dewan and Mr. Bajpai,' replied Jack. 'We'll give you the details in twenty-four hours. Of course, we shall need backup from Delhi.'

Jack, a mariner of high repute, had proved his mettle amply during his fifteen years in the Navy. But to plan and execute the escape of a marked diplomat and his family from a hostile country would be an extremely complex operation. He knew that besides the immense logistical support required for the mission, he would need a third eye to critically examine his plan and its viability. He spent the night mulling over who to confide in and take support from. Dorothy could sense his anxiety but decided to leave him alone—she knew Jack would overcome whatever it was and would not hesitate to seek her advice if the need arose. The next day, Jack shared his thoughts with Amar Singh, the First Secretary, who willingly offered to support him. Amar Singh was an IPS officer with astute knowledge of how the intelligence agencies functioned. Even so, they found it hard to come up with a workable idea. Soon, it was lunchtime, and their plan, in its present state, looked like a 'no plan.' Over a quiet meal, they continued to mull over their options. Dewan joined them, and while a million thoughts ran through their minds, none generated the confidence of infallibility and seamless execution.

Jack had the gift of being able to rein in his anxiety, no matter how hard a challenge was. He finished his meal, took leave of Amar, and walked back to his office with Prem. He stepped onto the balcony and lit up a cigarette to calm his nerves. Then he returned to his table and called out to his secretary to fetch him a set of detailed maps of Pakistan, Karachi, Sindh, Gujarat, Rajasthan, and Punjab.

India and Pakistan had a porous border those days, unlike the heavily fortified one that exists today. There were few check-posts and no round-the-clock patrolling on both sides.

Jack and Prem pored over the maps with microscopic precision. They could not afford to involve anyone else for fear that information could leak out, which would not only be detrimental but catastrophic for the mission. It became clear from the outset that leaving Pakistan by air was fraught with danger and a 'no go.' The Pakistani Immigration would be more than prepared to apprehend and detain Prem. The borders would have been sealed to deter any unauthorised exit out of Pakistan whether by air, road, rail, and even by sea. The idea of Prem leaving by a fishing boat appeared plausible. But the risk of entering Indian waters for a Pakistani fisherman was not an attractive proposition in the wake of the recently agreed ceasefire and heightened surveillance by the Indian Navy.

Eventually, after ruling out all other alternatives, travel by road appeared to be the least dangerous option; 'dangerous,' of course, being a relative term. To achieve that it would be necessary to travel by night. In the early hours of dawn Prem would have to veer off the road, wherever required, on a dirt track and drive over the desert, especially from Badin in Pakistan to the Indian check-post at Lakhpat at the border in Gujarat.

Jack pressed the buzzer on the intercom. 'Amar, can you step in for a moment please.'

'Sure, Jack.'

He joined Jack and Prem, who were deep in conversation over map routes and logistics.

'Amar, we have decided that the best option is over land via Baadin,' said Jack. 'You mentioned that we have a contact in Karachi who can help us cross the border. Can we reach him?'

'Yes, of course,' said Amar. 'There are a bunch of guys who polish shoes outside the Karachi railway station. The guy with a green coloured shoebox with a red star painted on it is our man. Go to him, get your shoes polished and mention 'Iqbal se baat karna hai.' Then go and sit on one of the benches in the railway station. He will come and meet you.'

'That's great, Amar. The plan is for them to go by jeep to Baadin and drive over the desert to Indian check-post at Lakhpat. I have taken the High Commissioner's clearance for our most trustworthy driver Prabhjyot to accompany Prem.

'As far as contacts are concerned, we have them in several villages and towns close to the border. I'll sound all of them out. But if Prem and Prabhjyot encounter some difficulty in getting to Baadin, do we have a Plan B,' asked Amar.

'Absolutely,' replied Jack, who had thought things through in meticulous detail. 'The terrain is vast and sandy, and there is a chance that the jeep might get stuck or break down. Should that happen, they will trek to Baadin on foot and join the camel caravan that leaves for India twice a week.'

Prem stiffened in his chair, understandably nervous.

'I know this will require immense caution and presence of mind,' said Jack, 'but it is our best bet. You are in good hands—Prabhjyot is as good as a local and can think on his feet. Prem, as long as you stay in the background, you are going to be fine.'

'I trust you completely, Jack,' said Prem, relaxing a bit. He wondered how he would conceal his identity from a sharp Pakistani official, if cornered. As if reading his mind, Jack elaborated on that exact point.

'Don't mind Prem, given your severe limitation with the language, you will be a clear giveaway the moment you speak. So, here is the cover-up story you are going to tell them if questioned—You are a non-Pakistani, an Arab immigrant from Somalia. Your name is Bashir Ali, born and brought up in a small town, Jowhar in Somalia as a parentless child. You worked in a landlord's house from your childhood, tending to his sheep and goats.

'Growing up, you earned the confidence of the landlord's wife and started doing household chores. Soon, the landlord chose you to be his personal attendant. He looked after you well and you led a reasonably comfortable life till you fell in love with the landlord's daughter and wanted to elope with her. The landlord got a wind of it and wanted you killed. You were lucky to escape in good time and ran away to the port city of Mogadishu, where you worked as a loader on the docks for six months. It was a life of hard labour, so you escaped in the next cargo ship out of Mogadishu and landed up in Karachi. There you were picked up by your master, Prabhjyot, to work in his warehouse. You are now accompanying him to Baadin on business.'

'One more thing: If somebody starts asking you questions on religion, tell them that you are not a devout Muslim and you have vague religious memories.'

'That sounds good,' admitted Prem, amazed at the thoroughness of Jack's planning. 'But please do not tell Nirmala Dewan about my second love,' he chuckled.

'So basically, we need ground support in Baadin,' said Amar. 'Ok, I'll get to the contact person and brief him in detail.'

'They are leaving tonight, Amar.'

'Sure! I'm out of here. Be back shortly.'

Prem and Jack went over the route in meticulous detail, memorising it till they were able to repeat it blindfolded. They both had to know the time Prem would be at each checkpoint for the final dash across the desert, covering a distance of approximately 200 km in five hours. The Indian High Commission had only one sturdy vehicle that could negotiate the rough and tumble of the desert road—the Willy's jeep manufactured by Mahindra.

They did not have the luxury of conducting a recce. Which meant that they had only one chance, and there was no scope for failure. Too much was at stake—diplomatic relations as well as precious lives.

After briefing the High Commissioner on the plans for Dewans' exit, Jack deputed a driver to take the jeep to the service station and give it a once-over. The oils, petrol, brake fluid and other essentials were to be checked and topped up.

The driver Prabhjyot, tall, muscular and bearded, could easily pass off for a Pathan. Bonus: he was fluent in Punjabi. Having worked at the High Commission for three years, he was also well-versed in the ways and manners of a Pakistani. Jack called him into the office.

'*Namaste* Sir,' said Prabhjyot as he stepped into Jack's office.

'Prabhjyot, *kaise ho aap?*' (How are you?)

'*Sab theek hai* Sir!'

'Family *aur bachhe theek hain?*' (All well with the family and the children?)

'Sir, *sab theek hain. Shukriya Saab.*' (All well, Sir, thank you.)

'Prabhjyot, *Ek zaroori kaam hai. Hum jaante hain ki yeh kaam aap se acchha aur koi nahin kar sakta.*' (There is an important task and I know that you are the best man for the job.)

'Sir,' said Prabhjyot, all attention.

Jack asked Prabhjyot to sit in the chair in front of him, took his hand in his own and swore him to secrecy. 'Not even your family should know what I am going to tell you,' said Jack. Though a bit startled, Prabhjyot gave his solemn promise to not breathe a word of the mission as long as he lived. Satisfied with the confidence that Prabhjyot displayed, Jack continued.

'We will give you the Willy's jeep along with a passenger to be ferried across the desert to India.'

'Sir.'

'Will you be able to do that?'

'Yes Sir. *Hum kar sakte hain*,' assured Prabhjyot. (Yes Sir, I can do this.) '*Zara route dekh sakte hain?*' (Can I see the route?)

'I will show you the maps, and the general direction of the drive. Keep the maps with you for reference, as we do not know for sure if these roads or routes are functional as of today. You will have to use your instincts to make decisions and adapt according to the situation.' Jack briefed him.

He showed Prabhjyot how to use the compass.

'Keep moving in the direction of Baadin and Lakhpat. Once you cross the border into India, show your documents at the check-post. Our contact there will have all your information. If you feel at any point you have to make changes to the plan, speak with your passenger and go ahead.'

'Sir, who would be coming with me,' enquired Prabhjyot.

Jack, well prepared for the query, buzzed Prem on the intercom, who joined them within a minute.

'Saab will come with you,' he said, pointing towards Prem.

Prem shook hands with Prabhjyot and pulled a chair next to him. All three began to go over the maps, discussing the main route, alternate routes and marking places where it would be safe to break path and go over the desert. It was also decided that should the vehicle break down or get stuck in the sand, it was to be abandoned and the original number plates were to be affixed, and the journey continued on foot or camel-back.

Jack had collected information about the five or six unmanned camel caravans that came over the border from India into Pakistan. They had been trudging across the desert overnight for decades, with the senior-most camel in the lead.

This, explained Jack, was the window that Prem and Prabhjyot would need to seize. Time was of the essence— the caravan stayed on Pakistani soil only for quick refreshments, offloading and reloading for the return trip to India.

Jack further instructed them to make sure they joined the caravan a bit away from the loading station, to avoid being spotted by the local police. The trick was to tempt the camels with chapatis, oats or leaves so that they would sit down for a while to eat. They would then mount the camels.

Prem, who had never ridden a camel, was told how to get on to one—to sit, the animal got on to its haunches, knelt forward on its front legs, rolled back onto its hind legs and then rocked forward. That was when you got on and gripped tight, or you could be tossed off.

Jack reminded Prabhjyot to periodically keep checking the compass, to ensure they were going in the correct direction. 'One wrong turn, and we're done for,' murmured Prem, a bit overwhelmed. 'Don't worry,' Jack reassured him. 'Look at it as a 200-kilometre journey that will take you about six hours, mostly under cover of the night.'

'I have complete faith in you, Jack,' said Prem, visibly relieved.

'Once you have reached Lakhpat, you will be in safe hands,' continued Jack. 'It is a small village fortified by a seven-kilometre wall. Our Border Security Force will have all your information and will escort you to the nearest airport or railway station.'

Once the plan had been vetted and gone over several times in detail, it was time to meet the High Commissioner and get his approval. Jack put forth his strategy in meticulous detail, starting with the fact that they had very little time and were up against the lurking danger from the enemy. He emphasised that road travel was their best, in fact only, option since the airport, seaport, railway station and bus terminals were heavily guarded in view of the recent hostilities.

The High Commissioner and Deputy Commissioner heard the briefing in grave silence.

At last, the High Commissioner remarked, 'I am sure this will work. All I want to say is, be fully alert at all times and do not panic if trouble hits. You will reach India safely.'

He directed that their personal documents be concealed in the sole of their shoes, and they be provided with Pakistani documents. Prem was to be given an adequate amount of Pakistani currency, which he could use to get out of tricky situations by greasing palms where necessary.

The mission was a 'go-go.'

Ever cautious, Amar Singh decided to go to the railway station in an auto-rickshaw, with his own car parked close by. He identified the shoe-polish boy by the green box with the red star and took off his shoe for polishing. While the young lad gave his already-shining shoe a good rub, Amar leaned forward and said, 'Iqbal se baat karna hai' (I want to speak to Iqbal).

The young guy looked up at him, took a few minutes to register the request, and nodded. 'Paanch minute mein aata hoon.' (I'll be back in five minutes).

Amar bought a newspaper and sat down on one of the benches. Soon, a young man in a Pathani suit approached him. Looking straight ahead, he said in a whisper 'Bulaaya, Saab?' (Did you ask for me?)

'Iqbal?'

'Iqbal Ansari.'

'Baadin mein itlaa kar do. Do parcel ko pahunchana hai doosri taraf.'(Pass the information to Baadin. Two parcels have to be transported to the other side.)

'Aap baithe rahein, mera ladka aa kar naam aur pataa de dega. Main baat kar loonga' (You please remain seated. My boy will come and give you the information and contact details).

Amar sat there for another half hour, then got restless and stood up, deciding to observe the bench from afar. Just then, the shoe polish boy called out, 'Saab aap ka roomaal gir gaya' (Sir you have dropped your handkerchief.)

Amar bent down to pick up the handkerchief. There was a note inside, on which was scribbled: Baadin Bus Stand, Chand Ghulam Paan, Superbrand 55*5. Amar put the handkerchief into his pocket, and walked briskly to the car park, happy that he had made contact and tied up all ends.

Back at the High Commission, he put the note on Jack's table. 'We're all set. Here is the name of the paan shop and the password.'

'Excellent. I think they are good to go,' said Jack. He called Prem and Prabhjyot and gave them a complete rundown on the contact person and the password.

The mission was a 'go-go,' but Jack's military training in ops told him that a decoy plan would have to be put into place. An idea was already brewing in his mind.

The Indian High Commission sent a courier with confidential mail to the Ministry of External Affairs every week. The mail was secured in a briefcase, cuffed to the wrist of the courier. They were accompanied by two security personnel to the airport and received also by two security personnel when they arrived in India. The keys for the cuff were with the Deputy High Commissioner in Karachi and the Secretary to the Minister in India.

This flight could be the ideal camouflage for Prem's escape plan.

He spoke to Amar, who listened to the plan with keen attention.

'The Swissair flight comes in tomorrow morning,' said Jack. 'We can make a provisional reservation for Prem so that his name pops up on the passenger manifest. The Pakistani agencies will be tipped off by the Airline. When they rush to apprehend him at the airport, they will find that only our courier guy has shown up for the flight. Meanwhile, Prem will have left Karachi far behind.'

'Superb, Jack!' said Amar. 'I'll have the reservations done before the airline office closes for the day. I'll also speak to Puri; he's taking the courier to Delhi this week.'

It was past 10.00 p.m. All the planning and arranging had left them exhausted. It was decided that Prem would spend the night at the High Commission, and the others would go home. As the High Commissioner left, Jack made eye contact with Prabhjyot, who was driving the car and gave him a thumbs-up, signalling that he was the man of the moment and must live by his promise. Prabhjyot flashed back a smile of reassurance at Jack and sped away.

They took care to maintain the appearance of routine work at the High Commission next day. Of course, each one of them knew and were waiting with bated breath for the night, when the mission would officially begin. At 7.00 p.m., all the staffers left the office, except Jack and Dewans. Prabhjyot dropped the High Commissioner home and returned to the office. All he had to do now was wait until it was time to reach the pickup point indicated by Jack.

Prem had a light meal at 8.00 p.m. and went to bed to catch a few winks before the post-midnight departure. At 1:30 a.m., Jack made himself a cup of coffee and went up to the room in which Prem was resting. He knocked gently on the door. Prem opened at once.

'Prem, it's time. Shall we move?'

'Yes Jack, let me make sure I have everything.'

Prem had a stoic calm about him as he quickly checked and gathered his belongings for the journey, most importantly his identity papers and the letter from the High Commissioner stating that he was an Indian citizen and had to be accorded protection.

Soon after, they both walked to the garage where the cars were parked. Jack advised Prem to crouch down between the back seat and the front seat of his car and covered him with a blanket. He took the driver's seat, turned the ignition on and drove the car towards the exit gate of the High Commission. The lone guard who was manning the gate opened it, too sleepy to carry out the usual identity checks.

Jack drove carefully, checking his rear-view mirror to detect anyone following. After driving around for about half an hour, he turned towards Karachi's famous Sadar Bazaar.

Even at 2.00 a.m, Sadar Bazaar was abuzz with the street vendors dishing up *sheekh kabab* and *roti*, a popular delicacy.

Jack parked the car in a small, dark by-lane. He asked Prem to remove the blanket. As decided, they got out of the car and began walking at a suitable distance from each other, with Prem in the lead and Jack following him a couple of paces behind. Soon, they spotted the Willy's jeep.

Prabhjyot, much like the local labourers, was sitting on his haunches some distance from the jeep. He spotted Prem and Jack and sauntered towards the vehicle. He was well cast into his new character, behaving nonchalantly yet cautiously. He quickly settled himself into the driver's seat, adjusted the cushion and his posture and turned the key into the ignition.

The engine sputtered in the cold of the night, and Prabhjyot pressed the accelerator gently, like a champion horse rider nudging his horse to get the best out of him. The engine warmed up to a steady hum. Meanwhile, Prem got into the seat next to him. The enigmatic smile on Prabhjyot's face assured Jack that the man and his machine were well up to the task and would not fail them. He smiled and sent out a silent prayer as he waved goodbye to Prem and Prabhjyot.

Jack turned and crossed the road. He walked casually to his car, without once glancing back at the departing jeep. He waited for some time before he approached the car, just to be sure it was not being watched. A few minutes later, he unlocked the car and drove quietly without switching on the headlights until he hit the main road towards Hindustan Court.

Jack did not want to be seen or logged in by the sentry at the gate, so he drove to the rear of the compound and parked the car in the shadowy recesses of the trees. His athletic frame and agility came to good use as he scrambled up the compound wall. He entered the house quietly from the rear door.

Dorothy, awakened by the click of the door, noticed Jack getting into bed and turned over to face him. He put his arm around her and dozed off due to sheer exhaustion. It was 4.00 a.m.

10

Across the Desert

Prabhjyot was wearing the traditional Pakistani attire of Pathani salwar kurta topped with a cloth turban with Turla (one end of the turban well starched and stretching about eight inches on top of the head) and Shamla (the other end of the turban stretching behind by about a foot on the back) a vanishing symbol of pride, nowadays worn by the Pakistan Rangers as a part of their uniform. His new leather sandals, beard and moustache completed the look of a well-to-do farmer or businessman.

Prem, stocky and dark-complexioned, usually wore a crisp white shirt and black trousers. But those would make him stick out like a sore thumb, so Jack advised him to get into local gear as well. Seeing him clad in a salwar kurta, sandals and turban would have elicited many an amused smile from family and friends, but of course the situation at that time was anything but amusing.

Prabhjyot and Prem drove quietly for the most part. And there were two reasons for that. Prem did not know Hindi, and Prabhjyot did not know English. Besides, the tension in the air was so thick, one could slice it with a knife. But they did manage to communicate with each other, relying mostly on sign language.

It was nearly 3.00 a.m, and pitch black. There was practically no traffic on the road. It was pretty chilly too. Both men had thick woollen blankets which they covered themselves with, and woollen scarves around their necks, but the wind still slapped against their faces in the open jeep.

There were no streetlights as they exited Karachi city. It was approximately 200 km from here to the border. Prabhjyot was driving at nearly 50 km per hour, and he was confident that he would be able to cover nearly 120 to 130 km before daylight. He could have sped but did not want to risk a mishap or a puncture. In those days, there were hardly any petrol pumps along the highway (if you could call it that), so the jeep was fully tanked up on diesel, and they were carrying top-up jerry cans too.

Jack had briefed Prem about the areas where the camel caravans came across from Gujarat in India. It was close to a small, remote town in Pakistan called Baadin, approximately 40 km to the border between India and Pakistan.

They drove along pretty uneventfully for most part of the journey. But just before a town called Makli, Prabhjyot noticed there was a long line up of vehicles. He suspected it was a check-post. So, he decided to stop a distance away and walk up to check. Sure enough, it was a police check-post. He returned to the vehicle and asked Prem, 'Sir, saamne check-post hai. Kya karna hai?' (Sir, there is a check-post in front. What should we do?)

Prem knew that they could not make it past the check-post—the documents provided to them by the High Commission were very basic. He asked Prabhjyot if they could get off the main road.

'Prabhjyot, jeep jaa sakta hai? Off-road? Kachcha rasta?' He asked, gesturing with his hands.

Prabhjyot understood and nodded.

The terrain was quite flat, but sandy. It was highly likely that that the vehicle would get stuck in the sand, but Prabhjyot was a highly skilled driver. He manoeuvred the jeep expertly, slowing down to just 10/15 km per hour. The border seemed agonisingly far now, but they had no other option and both of them knew this. They drove along the vast swathes of sand for almost an hour, hoping that they were going in the right direction. Prem had a compass and checked the coordinates frequently. They had to reach Baadin, but from a circumnavigation route. It was on the outskirts of the village that the camel caravans came in three times a week.

The sand was not hospitable to the vehicle, and despite Prabhjyot's best efforts, it slid off the path into a ditch. He tried to manoeuver it out but after struggling in a ditch for some time, turned towards Prem.

'Sir, gaadi not going.'

'Yes, I know,' Prem replied. He got out of the jeep, trying to collect his wits about him. Both of them tried to get the jeep out of the sand ditch, but the more they tried, the deeper the jeep sank into the sand. After trying for almost an hour, both of them realized that getting the vehicle out of the ditch would not be possible. Prem checked the coordinates of their location. He would send a message to Jack as soon as they reached India, and Jack could send a team to recover the vehicle. But for now, Prabhjyot and he would have to abandon the vehicle and resume their journey. Prem checked what he needed to take with him, and what they needed to leave behind. He had a small backpack. A few toiletries, a small towel, one pair of clothes. He also decided to carry the blanket with him, because it got very cold at night in the desert. Prabhjyot carried his blanket along, too, and with a bottle of water each, they started trekking towards Baadin. Checking constantly to see that they were heading in the right direction, they found a pathway, which made it easier to walk. They were still walking along for a few hours when a camel cart came along.

Prabhjyot hailed the camel cart driver. 'Kahaan jaa rahe hain, Bhai?'(Where are you going, brother?)

'Golarchi jaa rahe hain. Aa jaao. Main road tak chhod doonga' (I'm going to Golarchi. Come with me. I'll drop you off to the main road).

The camel cart driver, Daana, was a simpleton, and didn't ask too many questions. The pace of the camel cart was slow and jerky. Soon enough, Prem had been lulled into a doze. Prabhjyot kept a vigil. Both of them couldn't nap at the same time. Daana nodded off, too.

The sun was now at its zenith, spitting fire on the sand. The main thing was that they had managed to circumvent the check-post by dirt tracking, but they lost the vehicle in the bargain. Also, after walking for some hours across the desert, they had found a pathway. It definitely was not the main road, but it was a tarred road. It may have been a village road. Prabhjyot got talking with Daana. He got to know that the cart was on its way back to his village, after dropping off some goods to the local market. Prem checked on his compass. They appeared to be moving south and east. So that was a safe direction to be moving in.

The camel cart ambled along. And by 5.00 p.m., the weather got milder and the sun was much lower in the sky. Finally, they approached a tiny village on the outskirts of Golarchi, and Daana told Prabhjyot that this was as far as he was going. Prabhjyot asked him if there was any place they could stay the night and get something to eat.

'You can stay the night at my house, and my wife will make us some nice food,' he offered.' I'll give you two *chaarpaayees* (jute cots). You can sleep in the courtyard.'

'That will be more than enough for us,' said Prabhjyot and handed him two hundred rupees.

Daana secured his camel and the cart in a shed outside his house. There was enough straw for the camel to lie down in, and a water trough on the side. Daana hung some fodder in a bag around the camel's neck and walked clumsily into his house. There was a large courtyard, and a few cots arranged around the fire. An elderly man sat on one of the cots, smoking a hookah. It had a cylinder of water, some tobacco in a small container, and a pipe attached to it. It looked very similar to the contemporary 'sheesha.'

Daana greeted his father. 'Salaam alleykum Abba!'

The old man returned the greeting and asked Daana who Prem and Prabhjyot were. Daana replied that they were travelling to Baadin, and their vehicle had broken down, so they had hitched a ride with him. He explained that both of them were really tired, so he had offered to let them stay the night. They would be leaving in the morning.

The old man appeared to be satisfied with the explanation. And they never really had any guests visiting them anyhow, so some new faces were always welcome. Prabhjyot sat next to the old man and shared the hookah. The old man patted him on the back affectionately. Prem sat some distance away, playing with two dogs that were lounging under the cot. His inability to speak the local language would be a sure giveaway, so he sat at some distance and busied himself by writing something in his diary.

Soon, Daana's wife Shama served them vegetables in a curry with thick rotis. They hadn't eaten all day, so the fresh, hot meal was extremely satisfying. Afterwards, the men retired to their cots in the courtyard. A fire had been lit for them, and they sat around it, smoking the hookah. Prem did not smoke, so he lay down and covered himself with his blanket. Prabhjyot was in his element. He spoke the local language, so he was chatting away with everyone. He had just eaten a sumptuous meal and the hookah was the cherry on top of the icing. He felt invincible.

Daana lay back on his cot and covered himself with his blanket. Kahan jaayenge kal? ('Where will you be headed to tomorrow?')

'Hum dono Baadin jaa rahein hain. Kuch saamaan aa raha hai Kutch se, usko lene jaa rahe hain.' (Both of us are going to Baadin tomorrow. Some goods are coming from the Kutch area. We are going to collect it.)

'Baadin toh kaafi door hai—yahaan se kareeb 50 kilometre. Aur aap ke paas gaadi bhi nahin hai. (Baadin is quite far off. Another 50 kilometres from here. And you don't even have a vehicle.)

'Haan, woh toh hai. Yahaan se hum chal ke jaa sakte hain. Aur main road se koi gaadi mil jaayegi. Uss mein chadh ke Baadin pahunch jaayenge.(Yes, that's true. But we can walk from here to the main road. And there's bound to be a truck or bus we can hitch a ride on. Don't worry.)

Daana remained silent for a few minutes. By that time, Prem had fallen asleep. It was nearly October, and the nights were getting cold. Prem drew his blanket over his head and fell into a deep slumber. The fire burnt strongly next to them, lending huge comfort to their weary limbs.

'Kya kehna hai aap ka, Abba?' Daana asked his father. 'Main inko lekar jaaon Baadin tak? Wahaan se saamaan bhi lete aa jaaunga.' (What do you think, Abba? I can take them to Baadin. And get some supplies for the village also.)

'Theek hai. Chale jaao. Subah Sarpanch se baat kar lo jaane se pehle. Shayad unko kuch chahiye hoga.' (I think that's ok. Have a word with the head of the village before you go. He may need something from there.)

'Theek hai, Abba.' (Okay, father.)

'Shukriya Daana. Badi meherbani aap ki.' (Thank you, Daana. It's very kind of you.) Prabhjyot spoke with genuine gratitude, because he had absolutely no clue as to how they were going to get to Baadin, where they had been told to make contact with a person in a paan shop. The shop owner would guide them to make their exit from Pakistan. It had all been neatly planned; by now, Jack would have tied up the backend contact to their sleeper cells, telling them to expect two Indian persons who would need assistance in exiting Pakistan. Prabhjyot had decided to give Daana a handsome amount at the end of the journey but decided to keep it to himself for now.

Prabhjyot shivered, wrapped his blanket tightly around himself and lay down. Soon enough he had drifted into a deep sleep, out of sheer exhaustion.

Daana and his father continued to chat for another ten or fifteen minutes, then the old man rolled over on his side and dozed off. Daana lay awake for some time, watching the stars in the sky twinkling like diamonds on a velvet sheet. He could hear his wife and mother pottering around the kitchen. By and by, the sounds from the house also faded, and the lanterns went off one by one. Daana also turned down his lantern, rolled over onto his side and fell asleep.

One lantern remained alight and flickered in the breeze that blew over the sandy dunes. Prem would turn from side to side, quelling the tempest that raged in his mind. He hadn't thought this entire thing through. Maybe there hadn't been enough time to do that. The Ministry of External Affairs had directed the High Commission to extradite him without delay. He had followed instructions, and in the planning, there had been no time to inform Nirmala. He couldn't call, because they couldn't speak over the phone. And he definitely could not leave the High Commission to go home. Jack and Amar Singh had done all the planning, set up the agents they needed to get in touch with. The High Commission had prepared the official protocol for Prem to be received when he arrived at the remote area in Gujarat. They had the identity of the personnel coming across, and the permissions and escort to be given. They were ready to check the two arrivals medically, and escort them safely to their homes in New Delhi. And here he was lying on a cot in the middle of the Thar Desert in Pakistan.

What was his family thinking? Were they afraid that he had abandoned them? Had they been safely extradited out of Pakistan? Were they safe? It was all up to Jack. He had promised Prem that he would get them out. These thoughts whirled inside Prem's mind. Restless, he kept gazing up at the sky, praying that an angel up there was looking out for his family. Somewhere after the clock struck 1.00 a.m., he fell asleep from sheer exhaustion.

By 5.00 a.m., the sky began to get light, and the rooster began to exercise his vocal cords. Gradually everyone awoke, and Daana's wife lit the kitchen fire. She served everyone tea in mud cups called *kullad*. Breakfast was fresh parantha bread stuffed with spicy potatoes, washed down with glasses of goat milk. She also packed some paranthas for them to take along.

Soon enough, the three men were on their way. Prem and Prabhjyot paid their respects to the old man and thanked him for his hospitality.

'Woh toh kuch bolta hi nahin hai,'(He does not say a word) the old man remarked about Prem, as they left the house.

The camel cart rattled away. The Sarpanch (Village Chief) asked Daana to collect some provisions for the village on his way back from Baadin. It was pleasant in the morning and the camel was also well rested. So he was away with a canter, making light of the journey.

Once they reached the road, there was not much traffic. A few buses and trucks, now and then, along the way. But that was it.

They reached Baadin in about four hours. It was a small town with a few houses and shops. A bus stand, a railway station, a police station, a post office, a small bank, a mosque, a government school. The Azaan rang out five times a day, calling the faithful to prayer. And children played gully cricket on the road.

Prabhjyot casually asked Daana if there was a police station in Baadin. Chatty as ever, Daana said there was, but the circle inspector, who had to look after five to six towns, only made rounds here once or twice a week. There were two or three hawaldaars on daily duty, keeping an eye on people and things. Prabhjyot and Prem exchanged glances, aware that they would have to keep their heads down to avoid being sighted by the policemen. Prabhjyot asked Daana to drop them off near the bus stand. He knew the paan shop was somewhere close by.

It was time to say goodbye to Daana. Prem and Prabhjyot gave him warm hugs, and Prabhjyot slipped six hundred rupees into his hand. Daana's eyes lit up.

'Shukriya bhai!' He couldn't believe his good fortune. Of course, he had no clue how vital he had been to an escape plan that involved two enemy countries.

Baadin was a very small town, and any stranger could be easily identified. Even though Prem was wearing a salwar kurta and turban, with a blanket slung across his shoulder for good measure, he did not blend into the background. Prabhjyot, tall, bearded and rustic, played his part to the T, and it helped that he spoke the rural Punjabi dialect with a twang.

They stepped into a small tea stall and took a table in the corner, where Prem sat facing the wall. Prabhjyot sat opposite him and ordered some food and two cups of tea. Prem spoke in a whisper. 'Prabhjyot, woh contact banana hai. Main idhar udhar nahin jaa sakta. Log mujhe dekh lenge. Aap jaa kar pataa lagaana.' (We have to make contact. I won't be able to move around too much. You can go around and try to make contact with our person.)

'Ji Sir.' (Ok Sir).

It was dangerous to leave Prem alone, so Prabhjyot advised him to visit the toilet at the back and stay there for as long as possible, so he could avoid coming face to face with new people entering the tea stall, or anyone who could be troublesome, like the Tehsildaar or the hawaldaar.

Prabhjyot made his way to the bus stand, walking close to the shops and trying to blend among the people. His keen eyes scanned the shops for Chand Ghulam Paan. The bus stand was located in a square, the busiest part of the small town. Besides bus passengers boarding and alighting, there were rickshaws, auto rickshaws, and a couple of taxis parked at one side of the square. People were buying produce from the wholesale shops and loading them into carts and lorries.

Prabhjyot sighted two hawaldaars marking their beat, walking around checking the lorries and carts, asking the drivers where they had come from and where they were going. He quickly turned and started walking in the opposite direction. Soon, he spotted the shop he had been looking for. Tucked away in a small by-lane, Chand Ghulam Paan was a tiny little kiosk. He sauntered up to it cautiously, glancing around to see if there was anyone looking in his direction.

'Ek paan banana bhai, saada.' (Please make a plain paan). He turned to face the road, took out the money to pay and also the slip of paper reading Super brand 55*5 to the man behind the counter.

The paan vendor took it equally casually, put it in the drawer and handed Prabhjyot the paan. Then he said, 'Oh achha. Aap hain. Woh khilonon ki dukaan par chale jaayein. Abba aap ka intezaar kar rahe hain. Unko bolo ke Yusuf ne bheja hai.' (Oh. So, it's you. Please go to the toy shop over there. Father is waiting for you. Just tell him Yusuf has sent you.) He pointed in the direction of the toy shop.

'Ji bahut achha' (Alright) said Prabhjyot and started to walk in the direction of the Toy shop, careful to stay out of sight. He found the shop and walked casually in.

'Jhunjhuna milega? Yusuf ne bheja hai.' (Do you have a rattle for sale? Yusuf has sent me).

The young man seated behind the cash counter did not respond, but there was an elderly man sitting on a cot near the entrance. 'Yusuf ne bheja hai?' (Has Yusuf sent you?)

'Ji.' (Yes)

'Theek hai. Mera ladka aap ka kaam kar dega.' (Fine, my boy will do your work.) The old man turned to the young man inside the shop and called out. 'Razaa, inko ghar le jaao, wahaan Ammi se kaho khaana bana de inke liye. Andar ka kamra saaf kar do, nahaane ke liye garam pani rakh do. Shaam ko jaayenge.'(Razaa, take Sir with you, tell your mother to prepare some food and clean up the room inside for them. Get the hot water for them to bathe. They will rest till the evening.)

'Theek hai, Abba.' (Ok Abba) The young man leapt off the counter and walked out, gesturing to Prabhjyot to follow him. 'Chalo Bhai Saab, main pahuncha doonga.' (Come with me)

'Mera dost chai ki dukaan par baitha hai. Main usko bula leta hoon.' (My friend is waiting at the tea shop near the Bus stand. I'll call him.)

'Chalo, ussko le kar chalte hain.' (Let's pick him up on the way.)

Both of them walked towards the tea shop, where Prem was still sitting with his back towards the entrance. He jumped when Prabhjyot put a hand on his shoulder.

A hawaldaar entered the tea shop just as Prem and Prabhjyot were about to get up. Prabhjyot grabbed Razaa's hand and pulled him close. He spoke in a whisper. 'Razaa, aap hawaldaar ka dhyaan uss taraf kar do. Saab aur hum peeche se nikalte hain. Baahar intezaar karenge' (Razaa, just distract the attention of the hawaldaar, Saab and I will leave from the back door. Meet us outside.)

Razaa nodded.

He sprang into action, greeting the hawaldaar and engaging him in small talk. Deftly, he guided the cop to a table that was to the other side of the stall. Prabhjyot and Prem moved swiftly and exited through the back towards the toilet. The main road was accessible from the back of the shop.

'Chalo Saab, we have to go to a safe house. It's too dangerous here. The hawaldaars are walking around. I have made contact with our man. He's told us to go to his house for a few hours, rest and have something to eat. He'll come at sunset to take us across.'

'Okay, let's go.' said Prem.

Razaa caught up with them as they were walking along outside.

'Arrey woh hawaldaar mujhe chhod nahin raha tha. Salaam alleykum, Saab.' (The hawaldaar was not allowing me to leave. I somehow managed to get away. Good day, Sir).

'Walekum Salaam,' replied Prem.

Razaa gave him a curious look. The man didn't look like a local. He was dark-skinned and too refined looking—clean-shaven, with neatly cut hair. But he didn't say anything; all he knew was that he had been assigned an important task, and it was his duty to complete it without a glitch.

Prem covered his chin with the end of the turban and tied the scarf high around his neck. He walked one step behind Prabhjyot, whose burly six-foot frame kept him well shielded.

Razaa took them down a small bylane, to a house with a large gate that was closed.

'Ammi, darwaza kholo. Razaa hoon.' (Mother, open the door. It's Razaa.)

Razaa's sister Ameena opened the gate. She was twelve years old, pretty as a peach, with dancing eyes.

'Ammi, yeh Saab log hain, Abba ke dost.'

Prem and Prabhjyot heard Razaa pass on his father's instructions, and his Ammi set about preparing food and the room for the guests. Obviously, she had not been taken into confidence, and assumed that they were friends of her husband stopping by for a while.

Having been on the road since early morning, Prem and Prabhjyot felt greatly refreshed after a wash. They were in an unknown place, amid unknown people, but Prem had infinite faith in Jack's plan. As long as they followed the directions, they would be safe. Just 50 km to go; but these would be the most crucial 50 kilometres of the perilous journey.

The ladies of the house cooked them a hearty meal, after which they lay down on the jute cots in their room. They were relaxed in body but still tense inside. The wait for the evening seemed endless. Around 7.00 p.m., and just after sunset, the old man ambled into the house. Razaa stood at the bedroom door and informed them that his father had come. They collected their things and came out. The old man gestured to them to sit next to him. He waved Razaa away, saying, 'Ammi se kaho chai bana ke le aana.' (Ask your mother to make some tea for us). As soon as Razaa was out of earshot, he told them:

'Karachi ke Saab se baat ho gayee hai. Mera ladka Yusuf abhi aata hoga. Woh aapko paar pahuncha dega. Border ke 1 km pehle woh aap ko chhod kar wapas aa jaayega. Aap usski baat ko dhyaan se sun lena aur jaisa kahe waisa karte chalna.' (I have spoken to the Sir from Karachi. And we know what has to be done. My son Yusuf will be coming now. He will take you across the border. Just follow his instructions. 1 km before the border, he will leave you and return. After that you can cross the border safely.)

Soon, Yusuf arrived, and greeted the two men warmly.

'Beta, inko paar le jaana hai. Tagda party hai.' (My son you have to take them across the border. They are important people.) 'Ji Abba,' said Yusuf. He freshened up, ate some food and declared that he was ready for the journey.

As they said their farewells, the old man tapped Prem on the shoulder, 'Yeh mera ladka hai. Aap ko paar le jaayega. Aap ghabrana nahin.' (He is my son. Don't worry, he'll take you across the border.)

They walked some distance from the house to a clearing. There were two camels seated next to each other, chewing cud nonchalantly. Yusuf climbed onto one, and asked Prem to join him. Prabhjyot climbed onto the other camel. The camels hauled themselves up and started walking in the direction Yusuf was directing them.

Yusuf asked Prem to cover himself up with the blanket, to avoid being seen or recognized. He led the camels to the periphery of the town, at the spot where the caravans came in and docked. He had found out that one caravan had come in this morning and was scheduled to return tonight. The caravans mostly travelled at night, because it was cooler.

As the camels ambled along, the Tehsildaar's vehicle appeared all of a sudden. He must have completed his rounds and was returning home. He stopped his jeep and called out in the dark, 'Kaun hai?' (Who goes by?)

'Salaam Saahib. Yusuf hoon. Chand Ghulam ka beta.' (Greetings Sir. I am Chand Ghulam's son, Yusuf.)

'Achha, achha. Kahaan jaa rahe ho?' (Ok Ok!! where are you going?)

'Chacha ko parle gaon chhodne jaa raha hoon.' (I'm going to drop my uncle to the next village.)

'Achha. Abba kaise hain? Khairiyat hai?' (Ok. How is your father. Hope all is well.)

'Ji hazoor. Khairiyat hai.' (Yes, Sir. All is well.)

The Tehsildaar stood for a few minutes and watched the camels pass.

Prem and Prabhjyot were glued to their saddles, heads down, hearts thumping wildly. It was up to Yusuf to steer them out of this. Yusuf clutched the saddle with all his strength. The blood had drained from his face, and his heart seemed to be skipping beats. With every ticking second, they hoped they had managed to escape the attention of the Tehsildaar. Those five to ten minutes were the longest they had ever experienced. Fortunately, the camels were unaware of any danger, and so they kept walking ahead without stopping, and carried them into safety.

At last, the Tehsildaar gathered his things from the vehicle and walked into the house. He was either too tired or too drunk after a long day.

The danger was behind them, and they could breathe easier.

The camels ambled along. Yusuf began playing a mouth organ. It eased the tension in the air, and made the quiet evening ride a pleasant one. In half an hour, the landscape changed. There were very few houses now, and dim lights twinkled in the distance. Soon, the sky turned pitch black.

Yusuf stopped the camels, jumped off the saddle and seated the camels down on to their haunches.' Aap utar jaayein,' he said to the two men. 'Yahaan par hum intezar karenge. Doosra karvaan yahan aa jaayega, tab hum uss ke saath mein jud jaayenge.' (You can get down here. We will wait for the other camel caravan to come, and then we'll join the caravan, and go together.)

They waited for another twenty to twenty-five minutes. At last, the tinkling of camel bells echoed in the stillness of the night. Yusuf stubbed his *beedi* out, and asked Prem and Prabhjyot to scramble back onto the camelbacks. He straddled his camel and tugged at the reins and waved at the rider of the lead camel as he came closer. Yusuf requested him if they could ride along with them, to which he readily agreed as they had their own camels, and having some company was always welcome. They waited for the camel caravan to pass, and then fell in step with the last one.

It wasn't long before the road ended, and the desert track began. Prem already had a sore back after the six-hour ride, so he chose to walk. But soon, he realized his folly as walking in the sand in sandals was extremely tedious, resulting in foot sores. After half an hour he mounted the camel again, preferring to endure the misery of a sore back. The weather was cold, and the three men huddled into their blankets, as they slowly trudged across the desert.

Just before sunrise, Prabhjyot sighted the first lights, which indicated they were reaching a residential area, possibly a village. When they were some distance short of it, Yusuf stopped the camel and asked Prem to get onto Prabhjyot's camel. 'Sahib, bas yahaan tak main aa sakta hoon. Aage aap ki sarhad hai. Chhota sa gaon hai, Lakhpat. Wahaan pehredaar se baat kar lena. Aap karvaan mein chalte rehna. Gaon pahunchte hi aap mehfooz ho jaayenge.' (Sir, I can only come till here. Your border is ahead. There will be border security force, you can speak to them. Let the camels be in the caravan, they will take you to the village, Lakhpat. Once you reach the village, you will be safe.)

Before Prem climbed onto Prabhjyot's camel, he handed Yusuf five hundred rupees.

'Shukriya Yusuf. Badi meherbani.' (Thank you, Yusuf. It was very kind of you to help us.) They waved their goodbyes to Yusuf.

Delighted with the cash, Yusuf smiled at them, waved and trotted away back to Pakistan.

The camel rejoined the caravan as they crossed the border into India.

11

The Great Escape—Part 2

The Dewan Family Leaves Pakistan

The secret of happiness is freedom, and the secret of freedom is courage.

—*Thucydides**

Jack was up and about by 8.00 a.m. The children were at home and playing with their baby brother, as the High Commission had not yet cleared them to go to school. Normally, Jack would start his day with Dorothy and the children, but today, he had too much on his mind.

The family sat down to a breakfast of semolina porridge, two half-boiled eggs with one buttered toast, and a cup of tea.

---

* Thucydides: Greek philosopher & historian 400 BC.

A man of frugal taste, Jack had had the same breakfast for as long as he could remember.

Momentarily relaxed, he spoke with the children about their long absence from school and asked them to go over the schoolwork with their mother. He permitted them to go to the cycle shop and hire two bikes for half the day. The children were thrilled—it was fun cycling around with their friend Priyanka, the Dewans' daughter, who had her own red-coloured tricycle.

After breakfast, Jack picked up his briefcase, gave Dorothy a hug and a kiss, and left. The couple's constant demonstration of affection in front of the children gave the family a deep sense of warmth and comfort. Walking out of the door, he called out to inform Debora that Priyanka would not be joining them for cycling, as she had a slight fever.

Jack walked to Amar Singh's house and requested him for a lift to the High Commission. Absorbed in his thoughts about Prem's family's impending escape, he chose not to tell Amar about the previous night's events.

They reached the office, and Jack walked across to where the other vehicles of the High Commission were parked. He identified one of the drivers on duty, asked him to pull out a car and drive him for some important work in the city. As they exited the gate, he told the driver to head to the place where he had parked his car the night before. Stopping some distance away, he asked the driver to head back to the High Commission. Next, Jack walked into a tiny shop selling stationery. The moment the driver was out of sight, he walked up to his own car, started the engine and returned to the High Commission.

'Congratulations, Jack,' said the High Commissioner, warmly. 'All seems to be going well thus far. Though I have not heard from any office back home, I am certain they are well and truly on their way to India. Must have been hard on you. Good Show.'

Jack thanked the High Commissioner. While soaking in the compliments, his mind was focused on getting the Dewan family to leave Pakistan at the earliest. They still didn't know that Prem had been repatriated to India.

He walked across to the Deputy High Commissioner's office. They spoke for a while. A letter requesting the extension of all privileges and safeguards to the family of a high-ranking Indian officer was typed, signed, sealed and handed over to Jack.

Jack's priority was to avoid arousing any kind of suspicion— the Dewan family exit from Pakistan had to be absolutely discreet. To maintain the illusion of normalcy, he decided to take them out for a movie that day and escort them to the harbour the next day.

Jack walked to the official parking, where his driver Muthu was deep cleaning his vehicle. Even generally, Jack preferred to use the official driver sparingly, so he could move around more freely and avoid unnecessary explanations. So, Muthu was not surprised when Jack told him to stay put and took the wheel himself.

Jack exited the High Commission and drove back to Hindustan Court. The Dewan family was at home—Prem's wife, Nirmala, fifteen-year-old son Rohit, sixteen-year-old Sunetra and six-year-old Priyanka.

Prem hadn't come home for two days, and Nirmala was beginning to get worried. She rushed to open the door when the doorbell rang, hoping to see Prem. Though a little disappointed to see a different face, she greeted Jack warmly. She and her husband respected and admired Jack for his affable, helpful nature.

'Hello, Nirmala!' said Jack.

'We were about to have lunch, our favourite idli and sambar. Would you like to join us?'

'Thank you for the kind offer, Nirmala, but I had an early lunch,' he replied.

'Ok, but please do come in.'

Jack followed her to the dining room, where the children were having lunch. Nirmala poured him some coffee.

Rohit got up and walked around the table to greet and shake Jack's hand.

'Hi Uncle Jack!' said the girls in a chorus.

'Hello! All of you are looking well. Hope you had a good night's rest.'

'Yes, Uncle Jack, but Appa didn't come home,' said Priyanka.

'Yes, I know. He had some urgent work to take care of in the city suburbs. Don't worry, he is fine and will be back soon. In fact, he called me and asked me to take you all to the movie *Born Free*. I know that you all, especially Priyanka, are very keen to watch that. Be ready for the movie this evening. I shall come with Aunty Dorothy and the kids, and we'll go to the movie together.'

'Yay! That sounds like a swell idea,' the girls shouted.

'Ok, I'll pick you up at 5:30 p.m. this evening,' said Jack as he got up to leave.

By 5 pm, they were all ready and waiting for Jack and Dorothy to take them to the movies.

The Shea family arrived at their place at the appointed time in two cars, one driven by Jack and the other by Muthu. They drove straight to Rex Theatre where *Born Free* was screening. Beautifully filmed in Africa, this was a story about a lioness, Elsa, rescued as a cub by a ranger and his wife and brought up on their farm to be released in the wild as she grew up. The story took a poignant turn when some years later Elsa returned to the farm with her two cubs to reunite with the ranger and his wife.

After the movie, Jack drove Nirmala and her children in his car while Dorothy and his children drove home in the High Commission car. Jack wanted the security personnel to observe that they had gone out of the compound with Jack and returned with him.

The next day, at about 12.00 p.m., Jack drove up to the Dewans' house. Nirmala was happy to see Jack, hoping for a message from or some information about Prem. She made a cup of home-brewed coffee for Jack as he sat chatting with the kids.

Jack took his final sip of the coffee, leaned back in his chair and said, 'I have to share something with you. Nothing to be alarmed about, just a little change from the routine.'

'Oh my goodness, Jack! What is it? Is Prem alright?' enquired Nirmala, her heart beating wildly.

'Don't worry Nirmala, this is not about Prem. This is about you all. Our government wants all families to return to India, as they feel it is not safe here. The men will remain here for some time until the Government of India takes a decision to retain the High Commission or to close it.'

The family listened to him quietly, hanging on to every word.

'You know that the Indian Prime Minister has passed away,' Jack continued. 'There is immense uncertainty all around, so the Government wants to play safe and secure its missions, especially in hostile countries.'

Nirmala, anxious about Prem's absence over the last two days with no information about his whereabouts, was befuddled at the sudden turn of events. She was speechless for a while. Her mind filled up with questions.

Was Jack saying that the family had to leave Pakistan? If so, when? In a day? A week? A fortnight? Or a month? And where was Prem? Was he joining them? Or would they have to go alone? How would she manage all this on her own?

Nirmala was a simple housewife, whose world revolved around her husband and her children. Prem had provided very well for the family and protected Nirmala from the ways of the world.

Jack understood Nirmala's state of mind. He spoke to her in a gentle but firm voice.

'The thing is, we have to leave now. Just take whatever is essential, your papers, jewellery and any other precious belongings. You have to travel light, a small bag with a change of clothes would be good. No suitcases!'

Nirmala gasped, 'What about the household things?'

'We'll take care of those later,' Jack assured her. 'But for now, once breakfast is over, let's just collect the essentials and leave. No rush, but the sooner the better.'

There was an eerie silence in the room as the family resigned to their fate, apprehensive about what lay ahead. Little

Priyanka, too young to comprehend the gravity of the situation, kept repeating to her mother, 'Why isn't Appa coming?'

The family left for their respective rooms to gather their belongings and put them in a small shoulder bag. Obviously, clothes were a big no. But school certificates, birth certificates, passports, memorabilia from parents and family had to be carried.

Sunetra picked a skirt and matching top that Prem had bought her for her last birthday. Nirmala wrestled with the heartbreaking thought of leaving her vintage Kanjeevaram silk sarees behind. But one set of clothes it had to be. They assembled in the living room with one small bag each.

'Nirmala, please make sure you have taken every essential item. There is no coming back here once we leave.'

All five of them sat down and reflected for a few minutes, but the sudden turn of events had put their thoughts in a whirl.

Nirmala locked the front door and handed the keys to Jack, who placed them in the dashboard of the car. Rohit sat with Jack in the front seat, while Nirmala and the girls sat in the rear. Priyanka sat near the window and chattered away innocently, unwittingly alleviating the anxiety.

Jack had recced the harbour area several times and was familiar with the general layout, including the moorings. The sentry at the gate to the harbour stopped the car. Jack flashed his diplomatic ID. The sentry made an entry in his register and allowed the car to pass through. Jack parked the car in the car park and asked everyone to get off.

'Ok, we shall leave the car here. Take everything with you.'

'Ok Jack,' Nirmala replied. 'I hope we won't get into any sort of trouble.'

'No, Nirmala, don't worry. We've taken care of everything. It should be smooth sailing.' He responded.

In his heart of hearts, Jack was not so sure. He had seen many a well-made plan fall prey to Murphy's Law. Moreover, he was facilitating the unauthorised deportation of a wanted diplomat's family from a hostile country. Getting caught could lead to catastrophic consequences. But there was no time to think or worry. He held Priyanka's hand and walked with the family.

After a brisk twenty-minute walk, a large merchant ship with Indian registration painted on the bough loomed up before them. They approached the vessel. It was a merchant ship, involved in loading and unloading containers of commercial products and cargo. This was an advantage because it did not attract much security.

There was a Tally Clerk, who recorded details of all vehicles loading containers on the cargo ship. A solitary security guard walked around, indifferent to the constant noise of tens of container vehicles milling around. An errant driver caught his attention, and while they were busy arguing, the small group saw their opportunity and slipped past him.

Jack walked up the gangway to the deck, and onward to the Master's cabin, Nirmala and the children in tow. He knocked on the cabin door. The Captain of the ship, Ajay Mishra, opened it.

'Good morning, Captain. I'm Jack Shea. We spoke last evening.'

'Good morning, Sir. It's my pleasure to have you aboard my ship. What can I do to help, Sir?' said the Captain.

Jack ushered in the Dewan family, who had dropped back a bit. They exchanged the greetings of the day and sat down. They were served tea and biscuits. After a few minutes, Jack walked the Captain to his desk and they sat across facing each other.

'I understand you have been briefed about the guests,' asked Jack.

The Captain said, with some hesitation, 'Sir, what I was informed, just prior to your arrival, is that I have to ensure safe passage of a parcel to Bombay. There was no mention of any guests or passengers.'

Jack was quiet for a while as he gathered his thoughts. He would have to convey the message very deftly without setting off any alarm or raising unnecessary panic. He spoke quietly and slowly, thinking it through as he went along.

'Captain, the Indian authorities want this situation to be handled with utmost discretion, on a strictly need-to-know basis. This is Mr. Prem Dewan family,' he said, pointing to Nirmala and the kids. 'He is a diplomat in our High Commission at Karachi. They are required to be given safe passage to Bombay at the earliest for which I have due authorisation from our Deputy High Commissioner.'

He handed over the letter to the Captain and continued, 'However, their names are not to be entered in the manifest. They will travel incognito. This is all the information that I have been briefed to share with you. The lesser you know about the situation the better it would be, from the official standpoint. Please allow the family to stay in the Owner's cabin and have all their meals served in the cabin by your steward, with preferably no contact with other crew members. It's a short journey so logistics will not be a challenge. I am sure the Dewan family will be eternally grateful to you for your cooperation and hospitality.'

Captain Mishra, flabbergasted at the realization that he had just been assigned a dangerous task, fell silent for a while. His mind oscillated between Yes and No. This was the last thing he had anticipated. He had read and enjoyed spy stories of great escapes but never imagined that he would be an accessory to one. But the fact was that the order had come from the highest echelons of the Indian Government. There was no way he could defy it.

Reading his thoughts, Jack said, 'Captain, don't overthink the situation. There is a bigger plan in play. It has all been well thought through at the highest level. Just go with the flow. No harm will come your way. Keep your lips sealed and your head cool until you reach Bombay. Once you are there, you will receive further instructions.'

Before the Captain could respond, Jack took his hand and gave it a firm shake. 'Have a safe passage Captain. Good luck and Godspeed.'

Captain Mishra managed a faint smile. Jack joined the family and put his arm around Nirmala. 'Don't worry, you will be safe,' he assured her. 'It is a short voyage, just two days. Once you are in Bombay, all of this will be behind you.'

With that, he left.

Nirmala and the children were on their own now, and she knew she had to remain strong for the sake of her family. She was grateful for her young son Rohit who, though just fifteen, was a pillar of strength to her. She looked at him and he looked back at her and squared his shoulders.

Shortly thereafter, Captain Mishra, gauging the apprehensions of the family, rang for his steward. A smart lad in his early twenties appeared from around the stairwell.

'Sir.'

'Nandu, please escort Madam and children to the Owner's cabin. They will be with us till Bombay. Arrange for their meals and ensure that they are comfortable.'

'Sir.'

Nandu waited for them to gather their belongings. He ushered them out of the Master's cabin and led the way to the Owner's cabin, much more luxurious than the Master's cabin. It had a large living area, attached dining area, a large bedroom with en suite shower. It was more than comfortable for the four of them.

Little Priyanka was thrilled to see a small movie projector in the living room. Nandu was more than happy to share the list of movies available on the ship. This was turning out to be a holiday in disguise. The spirits of the family lifted. Nirmala prevailed upon the children to eat before they could settle down to watch a movie.

She asked Nandu, 'Is it possible to arrange some food for us?

Nandu was quick to reply, 'Yes Ma'am. The cooks will have lunch ready in about twenty to thirty minutes. I will just go to the main kitchen and organize everything.'

He returned a short while later and began setting the dining table. Soon, a waiter entered the cabin with lunch. Nirmala and the children sat down at the dining table and ate in silence. The food was delicious, making the prospect of an after-meal movie all the more attractive.

Rohit, Priyanka and Sunetra settled into the plush sofa. Nandu switched on the projector, happy for the opportunity to sit comfortably and watch a movie. Nirmala was really not in the frame of mind to watch a movie, but the children insisted that she join them.

Fortunately, Nandu had selected an old Laurel and Hardy comedy called "Block-Heads". The cabin filled up with squeals of laughter. At the end of the movie, everyone felt better, with big smiles on their faces. Nandu brought tea for everyone, and they sat around the living room, chatting for hours.

'Good afternoon, Captain. All set to set sail?' The pilot greeted the Captain.

'Good afternoon,' Captain Mishra greeted the pilot. 'I am awaiting an all-clear from the Chief Officer to start up and depart.' He hoped his voice did not give a clue as to how anxious he was for a quick departure from Karachi Harbour.

Soon the Chief Officer came up to the Bridge accompanied by the Second Officer, who was carrying the cargo documents and the passenger manifest. It was no surprise that the names of Dewan family were unlisted. The Captain perused the dossier with due diligence and gave his nod.

Half an hour later, the Chief Officer gave the command for the engines to start up. As per procedure, the tugs tow the vessel out of the dock and the harbour, the engines of the ship are started and kept ready to take on, in case of any problem with the tugs. Usually, two tugs are attached to the ship by ropes or cables to tow the vessel away from the quay side and then out of the harbour. The tugs continue to tow and direct the ship into the mainstream. Thereafter, the ship uses its own power to set sail. Towing completed, the pilot got off the ship, onto the boat and gave a smart salute followed by a thumbs up, wishing them bon voyage.

The Captain returned the salute and gave the command to rev up the engines to accelerate to the required cruise speed. The ship had sailed just about two nautical miles away from Pakistan shore when the Captain noticed a Coast Guard vessel heading towards them. Normally, such a sighting would be treated as a routine affair. Today, however, the Captain was completely spooked. He shuddered to think of the consequences if they discovered that he was carrying stowaways.

He maintained the ship's pace and course without faltering. The Coast Guard boat noticed the Indian flag on the bough of the ship and moved closer to investigate. One of the crew hollered on the megaphone to ask for the registration information of the ship. The Chief Officer, who was on the Bridge, conveyed them on the megaphone—the name of the vessel, place and date of registration, the year of manufacture and the type of vessel and cargo.

After what seemed an eternity, the Coast Guard boat began to veer away from the ship. Watching it sail away was the most delightful sight that the Captain had seen in a long time. He asked the engineer to boost the engines full steam ahead. All they needed to do now was to get out of Pakistan's territorial waters at the earliest. Once the ship reached the international waters, Captain Mishra breathed a sigh of relief. He tried to busy himself with routine paperwork, but inside his uniform, his heart continued to beat fast.

By about 7 pm, the ship was sailing steadily in the calm Arabian Sea. Captain Mishra walked into the Owner's cabin to check on his guests and was pleased to learn that the family had been well looked after. He spoke with Nirmala for a while. 'At sea, we run a shift system when we are sailing,' he told her. 'One of the senior officers has to be on the Bridge at all times. Besides, a round-the-clock manning is done by the engineers in the engine room and the mariner behind the wheel. The shift starts at 8 p.m. and continues till 12.00 p.m. The next shift is from 12.00 a.m. to 4.00 a.m., and then from 4.00 a.m. to 8.00 a.m. So, we have an early dinner around 7.00 p.m., sleep early and rise early.'

'Wow! That sounds awesome,' said Rohit

'You can come up to the Bridge if you . . .' and then the Captain stopped short in mid-sentence. He realized there would be other crew members on the Bridge and he would not be able to justify Rohit's presence. He changed tack, 'I'll send Nandu up to fetch you if I can admit you on the Bridge; but don't set your hopes high'.

Nirmala inadvertently came to the Captain's rescue. She was reluctant to send her son out of the cabin. 'Thank you so much for your kind offer, Captain, but we have had a long and tiring day. It's best that we have dinner and turn in early for the night.'

'That settles it then, Rohit. It'll be dinner and an early night for you,' said the Captain. Wishing them a restful night, he walked out.

Food on the ship was delectable. It was always a challenge to keep the crew motivated as most of them were on contract, and sailing for extended periods without their families. Sometimes, the voyage entailed weeks at sea and nobody was permitted to drink alcohol when the ship was sailing. The quality and variety of the food had to be excellent to compensate for all of this. The cooks prided themselves on their culinary skills. After all, good food went a long way in keeping a happy ship.

They woke up to a calm sea and a gentle breeze blowing in from the west. Nandu walked in with a wholesome breakfast. The day passed uneventfully for the family as the children kept themselves busy, playing carom, reading books and chuckling at comics.

Occasionally, the Captain checked on them to see if everything was okay. He informed Nirmala that they would be docking in Bombay the next day but was not sure when they would be allotted a berth and could go alongside the Bombay Harbour, where they would offload. Of course, what he did not tell her was that he really did not know what their disposal was. All he knew was that he had to wait for instructions from the authorities.

The ship anchored at around 10.00 a.m. after forty hours of sailing and the engines were idling quietly. After two days, there was a stillness about the ship. The sea was placid, lapping gently against the bough.

Nirmala woke up first and decided to take a shower before the children woke up. She took out a nice saree to wear from the small bag she had carried. She knew it would be a significant day for them to step into their country, out of the jaws of an enemy state. The last couple of days had been hectic and traumatic, especially in the absence of Prem.

Soon the children were awake. Rohit looked out of the porthole and noticed that the ship was stationary. Then he saw the skyline of Bombay in the distance, and his heart leapt with joy. They were back in India!

Nandu came to serve breakfast, feeling a little wistful that they would be leaving the ship. He had enjoyed their company. The childlike banter between them reminded him of his home, his mother and his siblings. *Oh well! All good things must come to an end,* he thought, and so would this short and affectionate association.

After breakfast, they got their belongings together to prepare for departure. But no information was forthcoming. Each minute felt like an eternity. A few hours passed. By now, a cloud of gloom had descended on the small family of four. They slouched into their chairs and resigned themselves to waiting indefinitely. Only Rohit could not sit. He kept pacing the floor restlessly, peering out of the porthole every few minutes, trying to detect some activity, but all he heard was the stillness of the ocean and the gentle thrum of the generators.

The hours dragged on. After lunch, they decided it was best to take a brief siesta to relieve the agony of ceaseless waiting. At last, while Captain Mishra sat sipping his evening cup of tea, the radio officer came up to the Master's cabin with a message. It stated briefly 'Make preparations for parcel to be offloaded at 5.00 p.m. Comply with all instructions.'

Captain Mishra read the cryptic message several times to ensure that he had not missed anything. He was relieved that the concerned authorities were seized of the Dewan family's presence on his ship. He glanced at his watch. It was 4.30 p.m. He made his way to the Owner's cabin, knocked on the door and entered.

'Hello! How are you doing today? I hope the journey was comfortable. This ship is not fully geared up for passengers, as it's a merchant ship for carrying cargo. I hope Nandu was able to look after you.'

'Thank you, Captain, we were very well looked after, and the food was excellent, especially the fish curry. You have been very kind and gracious.'

'You're welcome, Ma'am. Just wanted to tell you to get your things together. I have received a message that the authorities will be in touch with us in half an hour. We'll take it forward from there.'

'Oh, alright,' replied Nirmala, deeply relieved. The long wait for disembarkation had filled her with anxiety and misgivings.

Captain Mishra sauntered up to the Bridge to see what was happening. He noticed a small motorboat in the distance making its way to the ship. He fetched a pair of binoculars from the chart room and trained it on the boat. It could be the boat to pick up the Dewan family or a boat to take some crew members ashore. Nevertheless, they needed to lower the gangway so that some people could go ashore.

'Kumar, can you inform the deck crew to lower the gangway; looks like there is a motorboat headed this way,' he spoke to the duty officer.

'Sir, could the crew be allowed to go ashore?' asked Kumar.

'Hmmm, maybe . . .' The Captain trailed off but in his mind, he was hoping that it would be the boat to transport the family. The gangway was lowered to facilitate the crew to get off the ship and board the boat. But as the small motorboat approached the ship and came alongside, two smartly dressed men, who appeared to be in their thirties, stepped out. One of them spoke to the pilot of the boat, and they nodded their agreement. One after the other they climbed the gangway and boarded the ship.

'Can you show me to the Master's cabin?' one of them asked a crew member standing near him.

'Yes sure,' he replied and walked with them to the Master's cabin. They knocked on the door and entered, but Captain Mishra was not there. The crew member asked the two men to be seated and that he would get a message to the Captain that he had visitors.

Both of them were seated in the day room. When Captain Mishra entered, they shook hands and introduced themselves.

'Captain Ajay Mishra.'

'Sir, Alok Tiwari, Under Secretary, MEA.'

'Sir, Chandan Agarwal, Port Trust of India.'

'Pleasure to meet you gentlemen,' said the Captain. 'What can I get you? Some tea or coffee? Or refreshments?' Captain Mishra buzzed Nandu, who appeared in a flash and rushed to organize coffee and snacks. He was also told to inform the Dewans that they they should be ready to depart in a short while. It wasn't long before the two men got up to take their leave. Captain asked Nandu to escort the family to the gangway and meet them there.

Nirmala thanked Captain Mishra profusely and made her way to the gangway. It wasn't very simple to go down for someone who hadn't used it earlier. She needed some assistance. Nandu and Rohit helped her down and onto the motorboat. The children were more agile and managed to climb down the gangway quite easily. Soon they were seated in the motorboat, the engine was revved up and they began making their way towards the Bombay shoreside.

They waved one last time to Captain Mishra and Nandu, who stood on the deck and watched them go. Everyone on the boat sat in silence and enjoyed the ride. After twenty-five minutes the boat sailed alongside a jetty in Bombay Harbour. Stepping out of the boat and onto the jetty was a cakewalk compared to scrambling down the high gangway onto the small motorboat, with the waves rocking the motorboat and making it all the more difficult to get in. Alok and Chandan helped the family off the boat and the small group began to walk towards a structure, which looked like a reception area.

A shadowy figure stepped out of the entrance, dressed in a crisp white shirt and black trousers. Priyanka started to run towards him, squealing 'Appa!' Prem opened his arms and caught her in an embrace. Within moments Sunetra and Rohit had their arms around their beloved father. The four of them hugged each other for what seemed like an eternity. Nirmala watched them quietly, tears welling up in her eyes and a prayer of gratitude filling her heart.

Alok and Chandan stood quietly at a distance. They gave the family their time to absorb the impact of the events of the last seventy-two hours, which had been nerve-wracking. A minor error or slip-up could have culminated in a catastrophe of gigantic proportions with possible loss of lives or lifelong incarceration in Pakistan.

After a while, Nirmala went closer to her husband and slid her arms around him. They wept and held on to each other like there was no tomorrow.

12

The Cover-Up

Anyone can lead when times are great. The great ones lead when things fall apart.

*—Anon**

Sleuths of the Pakistani ISI continued their unabated vigil of the Indian High Commission. Occasionally they would contact their informer inside the High Commission for an update. But there was a complete blackout of information on Prem Dewan, including his record of entry or exit at the gate. They were waiting impatiently for him to exit the High Commission and arrest him for espionage. The arrest warrant had been issued, it only had to be served. At the end of seventy-two hours, the

---

* Anonymous.

sleuths were at their wits' end trying to figure out what had happened to Prem Dewan. Despite the strict vigil, he had fallen off their radar leaving no trace. It was decided to reinforce the surveillance around Hindustan Court, the residence of Prem Dewan. Even there they drew a blank with regard to any information on him.

Six families lived in two large colonial bungalows, so it was difficult to track the movement of all resident members. Their hope of locating Prem dimmed further when after three days the sentry reported that not only he but none of his family members had been seen in the courtyard for over two days. This was corroborated by the housemaid, when queried by the sentry, as she confirmed that their house had been locked for over two days.

Captain Taufeeq Chaudhry of the ISI who was deputed to serve the arrest warrant on Mr Prem Dewan made his way to the Divisional Office of the ISI. He reported directly to Major Moinuddin Malik, who was covering the Indian Diplomats stationed in Karachi. In Pakistan, all official communication, whether verbal or written, was in the national language Urdu. Though predominantly controlled by the Punjab ethnic community, Pakistan had unilaterally adopted Urdu as the national language. Taufeeq addressed Moin as *Janaab* (Sir), a salutation used by junior officers in Pakistan to address their seniors. However, in the context of the Urdu language, this was a term used by the subservient courtiers to address the Mughal rulers, the nawabs (local aristocrats) and the zamindars (landlords) in the feudal medieval society.

'Janaab, we are not able to locate Prem Dewan. We have been keeping vigil for seventy-two hours at the High Commission as well as the residential area, the Hindustan Court, but he has not been seen either at the High Commission or at his residence. Unfortunately, we have not been successful in serving the arrest warrant and arrest him.'

Moin replied nonchalantly, 'Arrey, he couldn't have vanished into thin air. He must be lying low. Keep your eyes and ears open—he is sure to surface sooner than later.' That said, Moin trained his attention on some file he was going through.

Taufeeq saluted Moin smartly and replied, 'Janaab!'

He tucked Dewan's file under his arm and marched back to his desk. Taufeeq sat at a desk in a large room, dilapidated and dusty. An uninterrupted loud clatter of typewriters, the pungent smell of bidi smoke and the odour of unbathed captives filled the air in the room, making it unbearable for more than ten minutes. He put the file away into the drawer, closed it and thought to himself 'Janaab is not worried about this matter, so why should I beat myself up over it? He probably knows better than me, so we'll leave it to his discretion.'

It was a great relief for Jack to return to his routine work. Planning and executing the escape of Prem and his family back to India took a toll on his mental peace, but he was pleased that he had measured up to the task and the Dewan family was safely back in India.

The unannounced departure of the Dewans soon gave wind to rumours in Hindustan Court about their sudden disappearance, causing consternation amongst the hierarchy, especially the High Commissioner. It became apparent that a tenable explanation was essential to ward off any suspicion, should the Pakistani authorities raise an official query. Though

Jack drew comfort from his firm belief about the flawless escape of Prem and his family, he had niggling doubts about its secrecy. He felt an uncanny urgency to get a second opinion and walked up to Amar's cabin and knocked on his door. As he peeped in, he saw Amar was engrossed in reading some report. 'Hello Jack! Please sit down. I'll be done in a couple of minutes,' he said.

Jack lit a cigarette and amused himself with the round glass paperweight, turning it on its swollen head. It turned around smoothly creating a spectacular kaleidoscope of colours but failed to humour Amar, who remained silent.

Amar Singh closed the file, which had two bold red lines running diagonally across on the cover and TOP SECRET endorsed on top and bottom of the cover. He put the file in the drawer, locked it securely and looked up at Jack.

'My car is held up in the garage for repairs, so came to request you for a ride back home in yours,' said Jack.

'Of course, Jack, you're most welcome,' replied Amar.

They walked towards the parking lot, engaged in casual conversation, punctuated with laughter. As the car turned on the main road, Amar cleared his throat and said, 'Jack, there is some heat and speculation about the sudden disappearance of Prem.'

'From which quarters?' queried Jack.

'Just a ripple at the moment, but it's bound to gain momentum, considering there's an arrest warrant issued in his name. The foreign office may send an official note seeking clarity on the matter and take a headcount of Indian personnel in the High Commission.'

'Yes, I too have been thinking about it and feel that we should have a well-thought-out unanimous response ready in consultation with the High Commissioner,' replied Jack. 'We don't want to be caught on the backfoot.'

'Yes, undoubtedly,' replied Amar, 'the cover-up should be equally, if not more, well-planned than the operation.'

A common thought that nicked their brains on the way home was how on earth does one give a plausible explanation about the sudden disappearance of five people, belonging to the Indian High Commission, from Pakistan soil? They found no answers, as they were mentally drained after a long day's hard work.

As the car's tyres crunched on the gravel road leading into Hindustan Court, they decided to mull over it the next day, after a hearty meal and a good night's sleep. Amar parked the grey Mercedes Benz in the garage and the duo walked silently towards their homes.

'Good night, Amar, catch you in the morning,' Jack wished him.

'Good night, Jack. We'll talk at length in the morning,' replied Amar Singh.

'Yes indeed,' nodded Jack.

As he reached home, he gave Dorothy a warm hug and a peck on her cheek. Jack relished the thought of a private evening, so rare in the never-ending social milieu of the diplomatic fraternity. He changed into clothes for the night and retired to the veranda with a bohemian glass of Dimple Scotch Whiskey, ice and soda.

Dorothy could see him through the mesh door that remained closed to keep the mosquitoes out, sitting in a pensive and distant mood in the dark patch of the veranda, smoking and occasionally sipping his drink. She joined him after a while and sat next to him. Jack reached out for her hand, clutched it gently and they sat next to each other in silent communion, with their hands softly intertwined. Time seemed to have lost its relevance to the compassion that filled the air and their souls, till the bearer Ghulam Masih came and announced that dinner was served.

'What do we have for dinner today?' enquired Jack.

'It's lamb steak in brown sauce with vegetable sauté and dinner rolls. And Madam has prepared delicious caramel custard; the children really love it,' said Masih.

'Hmm . . .' said Jack, looking at Dorothy. 'I'm missing the kababs I used to eat as a child. My father would visit on the weekends and take me to the local dhabas in Agra. They made sheekh kababs on clay-lined iron pits called *sigris*, over burning hot charcoal. I only have to think of those kababs and my mouth starts watering. Just wanted to eat some spicy kababs today.'

The butler excused himself.

'Let's get the children and go. I believe there's a local eatery somewhere in Sadar Bazaar. I'm sure Muthu would know.'

'Ok, I'll get the children dressed,' said Dorothy.

The children were playing Ludo in their room.

'Daddy's taking us out for a drive and dinner,' she announced, smiling.

They leapt off the bed, delighted. Soon, they were downstairs, all set for their evening out. Muthu was waiting. Debora got one window seat and Jon grabbed the other. Jack sat in front, next to the driver.

'Muthu, do you know where they make sheekh kababs?'

Muthu, who preferred his idli-dosa, said vaguely, 'Sir, there are many places . . . but yes, I heard Rashid saying that there is a good one in Sadar Bazaar. It's a roadside cart, not a restaurant, though. Miyan Mirza is the name, Sir.'

'Yes, that's ok.'

Muthu drove along Karachi's main road towards Sadar Bazaar. Besides the local buses, the autorickshaws, there were designated tracks for the local trams, which moved slowly enough for passengers to jump on and off. The neon-lit signboard of Bambino Restaurant-cum-Night Club flashed an image of a girl with dancing hips, adding an air of romance to the ambience.

Muthu approached the Empress Market, Sadar Bazaar's shopping hub. Here is where the locals converged for all their daily needs—clothes, shoes, electronics, vegetables, meat, grocery, stationery, medicines. It was a magnificent 1889 building, designed by Sir James Ferguson and dedicated to Queen Victoria, then the reigning Empress of India. The building was arranged around a courtyard, known for its majestic clock tower and four galleries that housed more than 1000 shops.

Muthu parked the car on the side of the pavement, and the family got out. Jack walked with Jon and Debora on either side, holding hands. Dorothy walked beside them. The shops with toys and lights twinkled and the aroma of the kababs filled the air. The hustle and bustle of people shopping, chatting, eating and laughing was a wonderful change from the family's usually quiet environs.

Tucked away in the corridors of Empress market, away from the main road, stood Mirza Miyan's kabab stall. Skewers of juice-dripping sheekh kababs were turning on sigris. A large cast-iron pan was covered with flatbread called paranthas, the perfect accompaniment to kababs. The aroma was very appetising.

Memories of Agra, and the evenings he and his father shared, came wafting back to Jack. He wanted to relive those moments with his children.

'Kya bana rahe ho miyan?' (What's on the menu, Miyan?)

'Janaab, sheekh kabab, boti kabab, shaami kabab, chicken tikka. Paratha. Kya lenge aap?'

(What would you like to eat?)

'Chaar plate sheekh kabab aur paranthe.' (Four plates of sheekh kabab and parantha please.)

'Ji Janaab. Aap wahan chaarpaayee par baith jaayein. Ladka le aayega.' (Yes Sir. Please sit on those cots there. The waiter will bring it to you.)

Jack and the family sat on the chaarpaayee (a rustic jute-woven cot, usually for truck drivers to rest on for the night). In a flash, they were served four plates of sheekh kababs with onion rings on the side, and a dollop of mint chutney. Hot off the skewers, the kababs simply melted in their mouths. They ordered another round, managing to persuade Muthu to savour a plateful too.

Jack got up to pay the bill. 'Waah miyan aapke haath mein kya jaadu hai. Bahut mazedaar kabaab banaayein hain aap ne.' (Wow! Miyan, you have magic in your hands. The kababs you made are delicious.)

'Shukriya Saab. Aur koi Khidmat?' (Thank you, Sir. Can I do anything else for you?)

'Nahin bas, hisaab kariye.' (No thanks. Let me know how much to pay).

Jack settled the bill, and the small group left Mirza Miyan's stall to look around the shops.

'Phir se aana, Saab,' Miyan Mirza called out. (Please come again.)

After a spot of browsing around the colourful shops, they headed back to the car. Just then, Jack spotted a kulfi stall along Jehangir Park. He decided to give the children their first taste of kulfi with falooda. The creamy dessert, served with translucent rosewater-flavoured noodles, hit the bullseye, resulting in delighted smiles all around.

Muthu drove a very well-fed Shea family back to Hindustan Court.

They retired early for the night. Jack had a peaceful sleep and woke up fresh to combat a new set of challenges and possibilities.

The next day saw the High Commissioner, the Deputy High Commissioner, three Military Attachés, and the First Secretary congregate in the conference room that was stark, modest and occasionally debugged. In the 1960s the Indian High Commission was a modest outfit with the typical structure of a government building, prudent and socialistic in its appearance.

The men seated around the table were well aware of the subject of discussion and carried several jottings on their notepads as an aide memoir. The High Commissioner spoke first and set the tone of the meeting.

'Gentlemen, we have gathered here to discuss our strategy to tackle a contingency where one or more members of our country could be trapped and subjected to captivity in enemy territory. How would we handle such a situation? This is a hypothetical scenario and should not be confused with any other situation that may or may not have occurred. Yet it is to be given every importance considering all variables to make a viable plan of action.' The underlying message of this important statement was well clear to all.

Amar Singh took the discussion forward. 'This could be a complex operation as we will have to ensure no confrontation with the Pakistanis. They will use every means possible, including round-the-clock surveillance to establish who all were involved and what transpired. Persons suspected of involvement could face dire consequences to themselves, their family and their property, including harassment. So, our actions and response should not create an iota of doubt about the involvement of any of our members.' Amar turned in his chair to face the High Commissioner and continued, 'What can the State do in such circumstances to protect the people who have put their lives in extreme danger for the protection and safe passage of our fellow countrymen?'

The room fell silent, as everyone mulled over the significance of Amar Singh's words, loaded with pragmatism and Solomon's wisdom.

The High Commissioner responded, 'We are all aware of the untimely demise of the Prime Minister and that an interim Government is holding the fort. Considering that we are just coming out of a war with Pakistan, our High Commission here will have to be extremely cautious in all its dealings with the enemy state. There will be no room for indiscretion. The Ministry of External Affairs or the Government may not be able to offer us much support or assistance in an adversity.'

Jack chipped in, 'It appears to be a sink or swim scenario in a quagmire.'

'I'm afraid you read that well,' replied the High Commissioner.

'Given the situation, the most prudent move would be to maintain a low profile for some time. Play it by the ear, be alert, watch how the situation unfolds and keep the powder dry for any contingency.'

'There will probably be an enquiry. We may be questioned and asked for a credible response. Given that diplomatic immunity applies to all of us, they cannot officially apprehend us. Having said that, there is always the possibility of them using unethical practices to target us. We are not equipped to protect each one of us effectively. All I can say is that we must be alert at all times. These coming weeks and months will be critical for our survival.'

By now Amar Singh's spirits were somewhat dampened at the ambivalence of the High Commissioner.

'The direct backlash of such an operation will be borne by the persons who were involved in the planning and execution. It would be highly unethical and unfortunate to pull the carpet from under their feet now that the operation has been successfully completed,' he opined.

'That is correct but given the extraneous circumstances, the situation is way beyond our direct control,' replied Deputy High Commissioner Uma Bajpai.

Amar Singh responded animatedly. 'Sir, is it to be implied that such persons are to be left to their own resources?'

'The High Commission will extend its security to all persons who remain in its premises but, unfortunately, we do not have the wherewithal to extend that security once you step outside,' said the High Commissioner.

'That isn't saying much, Sir,' quipped Amar Singh. 'I am horrified. Someone has put his life on the line to rescue a compatriot, and now you throw him a salvo, saying you're on your own buddy. Take care!'

All this while, Jack was maintaining a stoic silence and pondering over the animated discussion, as he knew well that he would be in the eye of the storm if something of the kind actually happened. He interjected at this point. 'We'll probably have to set up some kind of a buddy system, to ensure that wherever we go we are in pairs and never alone. This will ensure that there would always be a mutual cover and if something unfortunate befalls, at the very least, someone would be at hand to help and alert the authorities. We can share our daily activities with each other and coordinate our movement.'

Jack's suggestion of a buddy system resonated well with all and they willingly concurred.

'Furthermore,' continued the High Commissioner, 'any explanation of the absence of the personnel must always have a common narrative. Anything repeated time and time again begins to assume the shape of a holy truth and doesn't take long for acceptance. So let us work on the narrative now. How should we go about it? What is the storyline to be followed?'

The Army Attaché, Brigadier Kamran, who served in the northern areas of Kashmir and had toured that area extensively, including the neighbouring areas in Pakistan, had something to offer. 'In the northern areas of Kashmir and neighbouring Pakistan, there are contiguous features, which are not very well defined by the watersheds and are common grazing grounds for nomads from both countries. It is another world for these nomads, aka 'Bakarwals,' who share common values and lifestyles and move unhindered from place to place for grazing their sheep. Unauthorised buses and trucks ply along the abandoned tracts and dirt roads in those areas. Though monitored by immigration authorities, they are not scrutinized meticulously. There is skeletal staff, not very stringent and quite amenable to greasing of the palms. We could build a story about trekking in this area by the missing persons, who perhaps fell victim to the elements or were taken captive by the locals for some ransom.'

'Are you confident this would work?' asked the High Commissioner.

'I am sanguine we could sell this narrative.'

'Do we have another line of approach? Any other ideas?' queried the High Commissioner.

'This appears to be the most plausible and convincing line that we all could pursue,' said Jack. 'Brigadier Kamran can get back to us in a few days with the latest status in that area and the feasibility of such an occurrence. Meanwhile, we will do some brainstorming and background check on the workability to confirm the narrative. We have to square our story to make sure everybody is on the same page.'

The High Commissioner, though somewhat circumspect, nodded in agreement. It was agreed that they would meet again after Brigadier Kamran got back to them with a feasibility report.

Everybody collected their papers. They had to be very careful about the notes scribbled during the meeting and ensure the room was well sanitized, as leaving any traces of written material could be a vital source of information to an interested party.

They all were happy that they had engaged in a successful mission, enabling the escape of Prem and his family. Yet a cloud of gloom hung in their hearts as they were apprehensive of an unforeseen eventuality.

There was no denying that the entire top echelon of the Indian High Commission would feel the heat if it was discovered that the family had disappeared from Pakistan, especially when an arrest warrant had been issued against Prem.

Pakistani authorities would leave no stone unturned to investigate the disappearance of Prem Dewan and his family, and details of the people who had facilitated that. There could be serious backlash for the person or persons involved in enabling the escape.

Everyone who walked out after the meeting that afternoon left the office at the same time and collectively drove home together, trying to stay as close together as they could. There was comfort in one another's presence. They were acutely aware that they were in an enemy country without much protection and had to exercise utmost care for self-protection.

13

Pakistan Closes In

Those who deny freedom to others, deserve it not for themselves;
and, under a just God, cannot long retain it.

—*Abraham Lincoln**

Taufeeq collected Prem Dewan' file yet again and marched to the office of his senior officer Moinuddin. He had been trying, in earnest, over the last four weeks to attract Moinuddin's attention to a matter he thought was of national importance, but to no avail. Mercifully, he had been spared the ignominy of a dressing down by Moinuddin. But today, he was determined to close the issue. He would either get a decision on the file or

---

* Abraham Lincoln, letter to H L Pierce, April 6, 1859.

forever consign it to the recesses of the dusty cupboard that was home to almost 500 other neglected files.

He knocked on the door to Moin's office but received no response, so he stood next to the door biding his time before a second knock. Craning his neck, he tried to hear the conversation inside. Moin was explaining something in a subservient tone. The other person sounded severe. Taufeeq heard a clatter of files falling to the floor, and heard Moin repeat '*Ji Janaab, Ji Janaab.*'

Taufeeq wondered whether to return to his office and come back another time or knock on the door to save his boss from the embarrassment he was being subjected to. He chose to leave for now. Pushing the file back into his drawer, he murmured 'Ab kuch nahin kar sakte! Chalo chhoddo' (Can't do anything now! Well, so be it).

Brigadier Kamran took more than a week to get back with the status report. His sources had confirmed that the road through Gilgit, north Pakistan, was not manned by immigration authorities, and showing an Indian passport at the check-post could get one across the border.

So, the narrative of Prem Dewan' exit was spun around their long-standing desire to go on a family sojourn in winter, to enjoy the pristine glory of the snow-laden Swat Valley and its surroundings. Since they would be moving around, there was no information on where they would stay. But one thing was certain, that they would return after three weeks. The story after three weeks would be that they just happened to cross the border and were apprehended when they tried to return to Pakistan.

Five weeks had gone by since Prem Dewan' file landed on Taufeeq's desk. Despite his concerted efforts, he made no headway with his boss to move the case forward. It was obviously on the low-priority list. He got busy with the mundane routine of sorting through files, typing out letters and responding to sundry complaints. The atmosphere in the office was dreary. Other sub-inspectors too were tied to their desks, doing exactly the same things as he was. 'Such drudgery . . .' he often muttered.

If there was one thing that broke the daily monotony with unfailing regularity, it was the 11.00 a.m. tea break. One could synchronise his watch with the arrival of the tea boy, who brought tea in small glasses, arrayed neatly in a thick wire holder with six slots. They sold tea in this rustic style at the local railway stations, and somehow, it made the beverage taste delicious.

Taufeeq took a sip of his tea and closed his eyes. When it came to tea, he was no less than a wine connoisseur. A peon approached his desk, 'Moin Saab bula rahein hain Janaab' (Moin Sahab is calling you, Sir).

'Theek hai, coming,' replied Taufeeq.

A thought struck him. Could Moin be calling him to greenlight action on Prem Dewan' case?! He pulled out a few files and walked up one floor to his boss's room.

'Come in.'

Taufeeq entered and saluted Moin. 'Janaab!'

'Is there any progress on the Prem Dewan case?'

'No Sir, I had come to meet you on this matter several times, but you said to hold on for some time.'

'How long has this been pending?'

146

'Janaab, an arrest warrant for espionage and anti-Pakistan activities had been issued in the name of Mr Prem Dewan five weeks back. Two of our agents had been deputed at the Indian High Commission to serve the warrant as soon as he came out of his office building or Hindustan Court. We kept round-the-clock vigil but there was no trace of him.'

'How long was the round-the-clock vigil maintained?'

'Janaab, it was for ninety-six hours. Thereafter, every once or twice a day there would be the routine information on the movement of all personnel in the High Commission.'

'When was Prem Dewan last seen?'

'Janaab, he was last sighted inside the High Commission on 5 October. All entry and exit records at the High Commission are maintained by the Indian security.'

'You do not have any inside information on those records?'

'I can work on that, Janaab.'

'Yes, we need to access those records. That will definitely give us some clue.'

'What about his family?'

'Janaab, ditto.'

'What!' screamed Moin in utter disbelief, 'That is alarming! Any official exit or entry from Pakistan of these people?'

'I will check and confirm, Janaab.'

'Get back to me on this in twenty-four hours. We may be required to expedite this matter. There are reports that Dewan has been sighted in New Delhi.'

'Janaab that was my biggest fear, that he may have been spirited out of Pakistan. Our suspicion was well-founded. He was an undercover agent of the intelligence wing from India.'

Moin frowned. 'It will be an unpardonable lapse on our part, should what you say is true. We have to move fast now. The Army Headquarters is breathing down our neck. Some kind of damage control will have to be done. We cannot allow the Indians to get away with this.'

'Ji Janaab. I will mobilise our resources immediately.'

'Alright Taufeeq, get to work. Take a jeep with the driver and an assistant of your choice along. You have three days to submit your report.'

Taufeeq left Moin's office with a spring in his step, as if he had been freed from a cage. This could be his moment of reckoning.

He summoned a young sub-inspector, Timur-ul-Shaikh, who was slow on the uptake and tardy in his approach to work.

'Timur, I want you to get information on the movement of all Indian personnel working in the High Commission. Get all the records for the last six weeks, especially of a man called Prem Dewan. When was he last seen? Where is he now? And any other information relevant to him.'

'Ji Janaab!' replied Timur.

'Take the jeep and the driver and report to me by the end of the day.'

Timur was off in a flash; anything to get out of the head office. He decided to go to the Indian High Commission. He stopped the jeep some distance away from the gate and walked casually up to the sentry post. The gate was manned by a Pakistani police officer and two regular guards of the Indian contingent. Timur signalled to the officer to step out. He came out of the post and they walked together for a while and shared a 555 cigarette, a rage in those days.

'Headquarters is looking for the movement register of all officials for the last two months. Try to obtain that by tomorrow. Give me a call when you have it.' Timur scribbled his office telephone number on a piece of paper. 'This is a high-priority task. Do it at the earliest.'

'Janaab, I'll see to it,' the police officer replied.

Timur shook the guard's hand and walked towards the jeep. He instructed the driver to drive to Hindustan Court. He conducted the routine exercise at all the premises and left his office telephone number for them to call him the following day. That done, he felt he had completed his work for the day and decided to stop by a wayside *dhaba* and have tea with the driver. They shared a few rural Punjabi jokes laced with expletives and laughed heartily.

Life could be fun, felt Timur, wondering why his bosses were so sullen most of the time. Anyway, now that he had joined the force, he had to role play and put up an appearance of working hard.

Meanwhile, Taufeeq was perusing Prem Dewan' file and some latest inputs that were received on him. He kept shaking his head and swearing in disbelief as he browsed through it. There were glaring lapses. Tertiary evidence that could help establish Dewan's doubtful antecedents had been overlooked, giving him a free run for espionage.

Sensitive information had been passed on to the Indian authorities, prior to the outbreak of the 1965 Indo-Pak war. It was clear that Prem Dewan had been the man at the helm of this operation. No wonder the Indian Armed Forces had been well prepared for an armed attack by Pakistan, thwarting their strategy of a surprise attack with consummate ease.

It was critical that they locate Dewan. Had the spy got a tip-off about his impending arrest and made good his escape before the Pakistani dragnet could close around him? The thought kept nagging at Taufeeq's head. If true, it would not only be a huge embarrassment for the Pakistani security establishment, but heads would roll.

Taufeeq well understood the futility of closing the stable door after the horse had bolted. So, he decided that the only way to mitigate the misery was to identify the personnel in the Indian High Commission who were complicit in Dewan's getaway. Through them, he would ferret out the modus operandi and the exact turn of events. India would pay for this, he resolved. Though the report would be prepared for Moinuddin, all facts would have to be presented by Taufeeq and his team.

Taufeeq was anxious to get his plan rolling at the earliest and waited impatiently for Timur to return with some inputs. Just then Timur ambled up to his table and began rattling off the activities of the day.

'Janaab, I went around the Indian High Commission, Shivaji Court and Hindustan Court, and one more residence for the Indians. Our security personnel will provide me with the movement records by tomorrow.'

Taufeeq flared up. 'We have already lost a lot of time in this investigation; five weeks have elapsed and there has been no action. Pursue these guys until they spill the information we require. If movement records are not available or have been destroyed, question our guards individually and repeatedly. Somebody is bound to remember something useful.'

'Ji Janaab,' replied Timur, with a look that betrayed lack of comprehension. Taufeeq immediately caught that look and yelled, 'Gadhaa saala (bloody donkey)! Do you not understand what I am saying?'

'No Janaab, uh! Ji Janaab! I got it. I have to collect the movement details of all Indian personnel from all their locations over the last two months, extending back to six months.'

Taufeeq nodded in the affirmative and dispersed Timur, who slunk away sullenly.

There was a lot to do. Taufeeq began diligently perusing all dossiers on Indian personnel received from the head office. While nothing in the files gave rise to any suspicion, something peculiar caught his eye. There was a significant number of movement records of the Naval Attaché, Captain Jack Shea, compared to the Army and Air Force Attachés. Jack, he inferred, must be a very active member of the High Commission. Taufeeq put the files away, deciding to carry them home.

After dinner that night, when all other family members had turned in for the day, Taufeeq sat in the veranda smoking a cigarette. He took out Captain Shea's dossier and read through it again. Yes, it did appear that the Captain was a very active member of the Indian community. Another difference he noticed was that most of the Indian personnel had sent their families home to India just before the war, but Jack had retained his family in Pakistan for no apparent reason.

Another red flag—the movement of most Indian personnel was confined to the High Commission and Hindustan Court. However, the same could not be said about the Naval Attaché. He would also take the family out for a picnic every Sunday to

Hawks Bay, a beach on the secluded and beautiful seashore on the outskirts of Karachi, quite far from the city.

Frequent trips to the market to procure provisions seemed reasonable and did not require scrutiny. Then there were frequent trips to the Harbour. He supposed these were fishing trips with the children, where again nothing unusual had been observed or reported. All the same, Taufeeq decided that it would be interesting to speak to the boatman who had taken them around.

There was more. Like everyone else, Jack Shea also went to his office in the High Commission every day. But even there, his movements were a bit different. He seemed to be staying back after office hours more often than the others. In addition, Jack's good looks, ramrod straight posture and soft-spoken demeanour gave him the advantage of being easy to like. Taufeeq knew Jack was someone he couldn't overlook.

For now, he decided to keep all three Military Attachés under the scanner, round the clock, irrespective of what he felt about Jack. He detailed another car with a driver and a staffer to follow them wherever they went.

Another diplomat of the Indian High Commission who drew Taufeeq's attention was the First Secretary, Amar Singh. He spent every waking hour with the Deputy High Commissioner at the office and then travelled with him to his residence and stayed there till after dinner. It appeared that something was cooking beyond the regular call of duty.

Taufeeq soon had his hands full with information that filtered in from various sources. His major challenge was to separate the wheat from the chaff. His own deputy, Timur, was neither very resourceful nor the most reliable.

The next day, Timur was near the garages at the ISI Headquarters at 7.00 a.m., preparing to go on the routine round of the Indian High Commission and the staff residences. The driver was cleaning the ramshackle jeep with water from a dented leaky bucket. Timur waited for him to complete the ritual and sauntered across the road to the tea shop. Walking back after finishing his tea, he saw a familiar figure at an unfamiliar hour near the garages. Instinctively, he bolted towards the jeep and found Taufeeq standing there in civilian clothes. Timur walked up to Taufeeq and gave him a salute.

'Where were you Timur? I've been looking for you for the last ten minutes.'

'Janaab I just went across the road to have a cup of tea while the jeep was being cleaned.'

'Yes, yes, that's alright. Can we leave now?'

'Janaab, will you accompany us?'

He dreaded the prospect of being stuck with Taufeeq and listening to his tirades and taunts. It was going to be a day-long ordeal. But there was no choice. Taufeeq climbed into the seat next to the driver, and Timur clambered into the back. They sped off towards the Indian High Commission. Taufeeq stopped the jeep at a vantage point, some distance away from the main gate of the High Commission, where they could get a good view of all vehicles that entered and exited.

'Timur, make a note of all the vehicles, the type, colour, registration number and person's name and designation. If you have difficulty in identifying anyone, ask me, I'll tell you who it is.'

'Ji Janaab.'

The High Commission vehicles did not stop long at the gate, so Timur kept bungling up the identification of staff, but carried on manfully.

Two hours slid by. Nothing much happened except a few vehicles entering the High Commission. There was practically no vehicle exiting and so no lead to follow. Taufeeq decided to go to the next destination; he turned towards Timur.

'Do we have anyone here?'

'No, Janaab. We have a constable positioned here but he is more or less ineffective, as the Indian authorities have isolated him from all matters related to their operations. He does not have access to the movement records of vehicles or staff except some sketchy snapshots from his memory.'

'Ok, call him to the office tomorrow after he has finished his shift.'

'There are four of them, Janaab. They work in rotation, eight-hour shifts.'

'Yes, I mean, all of them, individually, whenever they have completed their shift.'

'Ji Janaab.'

The jeep clattered along the potholed road, kicking up a cloud of dust in its wake.

They were en route to Shivaji Court and the Deputy High Commissioner's residence, adjacent to Shivaji Court. It was a large colonial bungalow with a plush lawn, staff quarters and security detailing at the entry and exit gates. Hindustan Court was where the Military Attachés and the First Secretary lived. Prem Dewan also stayed there.

'Janaab, we have a source inside the Deputy's house.' He meant the Deputy High Commissioner, of course.

Taufeeq cut him short because he did not want to discuss such matters in the presence of the driver. 'We'll discuss this matter later, Timur.'

The Deputy High Commissioner had already left for the High Commission. He was a bachelor, and therefore no significant movement.

Taufeeq decided to proceed to Hindustan Court.

'Timur, let's have a chat with the *chowkidaar* (watchman) who last saw the Dewan family.'

'Ji Janaab.' Timur leapt out of the jeep and walked around the block to the security gate shed. He gestured to the local guard, a pathan, to step outside.

Timur offered him a cigarette as they strolled around the block to meet Taufeeq, waiting in the jeep.

The chowkidaar saw Taufeeq sitting in the jeep and raised his hand in salutation.

'Janaab!'

Taufeeq asked him casual questions on the movement of the families and slowly homed in on the last sighting of the Dewan family.

'So which Military Saab was with them when you last saw them?' he asked.

'There are three Military Sahibs Janaab. I don't know their names, but I remember it was the *gora saab* (fair-skinned one) who drove them out in a white car.'

Taufeeq knew that the Army Attaché had a black Ambassador car and the Air Force Attaché had a blue Fiat car.

It was only the Naval Attaché who had a white Chevrolet, and so by all eliminations, it had to be the Naval Captain Jack Shea who was instrumental in the family getting away.

But this would need to be further confirmed. Also, by no stretch of the imagination could this have been a one-man show. The topmost levels had to be involved. But this was a start. Satisfied with the information, Taufeeq asked the guard to leave, cautioning him not to discuss the conversation with anyone.

'Keep your eyes and ears open. Report anything you see or hear which you find suspicious.'

'Janaab, I wanted to report several times, the children are creating such a nuisance . . .'

Taufeeq cut him short, 'Hmm . . . tell Timur about these complaints. He'll take care of them.' With that, they sped away.

After finishing a recce of all the locations on their checklist, they returned to the Headquarters for lunch and a breather. Taufeeq decided to write up the report of all the information he had collected that day. He felt good after a long time.

After lunch, Timur paced the veranda waiting for Taufeeq, so that they could continue with the recce. But Taufeeq did not appear. Timur peeked into Taufeeq's chamber and saw him bent over his typewriter, hitting the keys, oblivious to the cloud of smoke from the cigarettes in his ashtray.

'Well, I guess it's over for the day,' murmured Timur. He waited for the clock to strike 5.00 p.m. and left the office.

The next day, Taufeeq reached the office early. Moin arrived at 9:30 a.m., by which time Taufeeq felt he would burst with the news he had. He followed his boss into the cabin, feeling confident and energetic.

'Janaab, I have prepared a preliminary report. Kindly go through it and give further directions. The file is on the table.'

'I will go through it, Taufeeq,' Moin replied. 'I'll send for you. I have something urgent to attend to now.'

'Of course, Janaab,' said Taufeeq, trying not to let his disappointment show. There was no telling when Moin would look at the file. It could be days or weeks . . . one never knew.

There was nothing to do but wait it out. He returned to his table and began shuffling his papers around. It was no good. His heart was heavy and his mind was restless. He needed some diversion.

He cleared his desk of all the files and stored them in the drawer, put away the typewriter, closed up his desk and decided to look for Timur. 'Perhaps Timur is not yet back from his surveillance trip,' he thought. Nonetheless, he walked towards the garage. Sure enough, Timur and the vehicle were nowhere to be seen.

Where was Prem Dewan, he wondered for the hundredth time. How, when and where could he have gotten away? And who had assisted him in his escape? Undoubtedly the Indian High Commission was complicit in his getaway, but so far, they had not been able to gather a shred of evidence to implicate an individual, leave alone the entire High Commission. The only piece of information available was that the Dewans were last seen going out with Captain Jack Shea in his car. And they had returned with him later that night.

What was deeply mystifying was the complete lack of information on Jack's whereabouts, after he left Hindustan Court with the Dewans the next day. There was no trace of when Jack returned to the High Commission and there was a lack of clarity on whether they returned with him or not. Therefore, the information provided by the guard was somewhat tentative. Who knew, the family might still be in Pakistan!

Still, Taufeeq decided to follow the escape theory to its logical conclusion. He instructed six sub-inspectors to peruse all lists of flight departures, train departures, and departures by ship, as also road and bus departures over the last thirty days. The bus depots did not have passenger manifests so he called for lists of all Indian personnel, who crossed the border at various check-posts.

Taufeeq diligently and painstakingly went through all the information that Timur would collect daily. It was an arduous task that took many long hours.

The long days of hard work stretched into weeks that soon stretched into months, but there was no breakthrough. The data received from the airport, the railway station, and the border check-posts yielded nothing. Even the commercial passenger ships had no records of persons of those names leaving Karachi.

According to the information received from the main gate to Karachi Harbour, Jack Shea had entered the harbour every once a week to ten days. He always walked to the gate, so no vehicle registration number was recorded. His entry always read, Jack Shea plus two, or plus three, or plus four. Since he carried a diplomatic ID, he was generally not questioned.

There was no choice but to present the facts as they had been obtained and face the consequences, whatever they might be. Taufeeq walked into Moin's office, placed the file in front of him and stood silently. Moin opened the file. The opening page was the gist of the investigation report. It had two words written in bold letters that read, 'Findings Inconclusive.'

Moin couldn't believe his eyes. He blinked once, relooked at the page and sprang out of his chair as if a rocket booster had been fired under his seat.

'You moron, you took over three months to investigate and furnish a report, and this is what you produce! "Inconclusive findings!"'

Taufeeq was literally cowering in fear. He knew Moin wouldn't take it kindly. 'Janaab! The fugitives have left no evidence, no trail and no lead to follow. The entire operation appears to have been planned and conducted behind an iron curtain of secrecy and executed with clockwork precision.'

'Oh, shut up! I did not depute you to discover how good their plan was, or how well they carried it out. You were supposed to find the culprits. Utterly incompetent and third-rate job. If there is nothing more for you to say, you may leave.'

Moin closed the file and slammed the paperweight on the table. It rolled off and fell on Taufeeq's foot, making him wince.

'Janaab,' Taufeeq whispered under his breath and quietly exited the office. He sat at his table, distraught and staring into oblivion, awaiting the lunch hour. As the clock struck one, Taufeeq rose from his chair with his bag in hand and left the office for the day.

14

The Plan Unfolds

A man who has committed a mistake and doesn't correct it is committing another mistake.

—*Confucius**

It took a few days for Taufeeq to recover from his dressing down, followed by a nasty bout of flu. It took him a week to find the strength to go back to the office. Nothing more was said about the investigation report he had submitted.

It was for Moin to present the report to his superiors. The time had come. Every two weeks, there was a meeting of the Heads of various departments including Administration, Accounts, Internal Security and External Affairs. The Indian

---

* Confucius, Chinese philosopher & reformer 551 BC to 479 BC.

High Commission was under Moin's charge, so his report was the most eagerly awaited, especially since the two countries had just been through a war and one of the Indian diplomats, a suspected intelligence agent, had made good his escape from Pakistan. The information he carried could be crucial for the security of Pakistan.

Pakistan was under martial law at that time, so the external and internal security was assigned to two senior Generals, who were directly responsible and accountable to the President, General Ayub Khan.

The meeting, chaired by the General responsible for Internal Security began in earnest, with the various Heads of Departments reporting matters under their jurisdiction. Moin felt out of place attending a highly classified meeting where he, the sole Major, was the only one below the rank of Brigadier. Though it gave him a high, he was frightfully nervous.

'Janaab, we have been following some leads for the past few months about the sudden disappearance of Mr Prem Dewan from the Indian High Commission,' he began. 'We received reliable information that he was an agent of India's intelligence agency, working in Pakistan, under the garb of a diplomat, First Secretary Political Affairs. He came to Pakistan one year prior to the August war with India. We believe that he passed on some critical intelligence on our war plans to New Delhi, as a result of which the Indian Army was well prepared with counter-action when our forces attacked, resulting in massive losses and setbacks to us.'

He paused to scan the grim faces all around, then continued. 'The Ministry of Interior issued a warrant for his arrest on grounds of espionage. We reached the High Commission to arrest him but did not find him there. Nor has he been seen since then. Our personnel kept the High Commission under round-the-clock surveillance for over seventy-two hours but have not been able to make any headway.'

He cleared his throat. What he was going to say next would not be received well. 'Er . . . Prem Dewan' family, a wife and three children, also managed to get away. We are not able to detect or ascertain the time, place and source of their departure. We do not have any information on their current whereabouts either.'

The General stared incredulously at Moin, 'You can't be serious!'

Moin hung his head, murmuring 'Janaab.'

'This is just not acceptable Moin! We will look like fools if I present such feedback to General Sahib!'

Brigadier Aslam Sheikh spoke up, 'Janaab, I totally agree. This report stinks of incompetence and tardiness. General Sahib will be furious. More so, it will make us a laughing stock, the world over, if it ever leaks out. We have to create a different narrative. The Indians must pay for their machinations.'

'Yes. And it has to be something with significant impact,' echoed the General. 'Of course, we must ensure total secrecy, so that the trail never reaches our doorstep. I think you all can understand what I am saying.'

'Ji Janaab,' came the chorus.

'So put your heads together and work on a plan. Let me know in a week. I shall run it past General Sahib for approval.'

'Janaab,' said Sheikh. The meeting was dismissed, but the participants were too excited to leave immediately. They hung around in the corridors, discussing their ideas over tea and smokes.

Brigadier Aslam Sheikh stopped next to Moin, 'Drop by my office for further discussion, I'll involve some more people for assistance.'

'Ji Janaab,' Moin replied.

Brigadier Aslam's office was large and well-appointed. The wall behind his chair was adorned with General Ayub Khan's photograph in a golden frame. The Pakistan national flag and the Army flag were strung on their staffs, embedded in a gleaming wooden stand. Antique swords and weapons of the medieval era, reminiscent of the Mughal Empire, were displayed in a shiny brass showcase.

Moin sat across the Brigadier in rapt attention. Two more officers of Colonel rank joined them. Moin, a Major, was the junior most in the room.

Brigadier Aslam leafed through Moin's report, pausing to toss a query or two. Finally, he closed the file and said, 'How does an Indian diplomat suddenly disappear from Karachi? Do we not keep an eye on their movements?'

Moin shifted uncomfortably in his chair. 'Yes, we do Janaab. Regrettably, there have been some glaring lapses in our intelligence and surveillance.'

'That is disgraceful, sleeping on the job! Unbelievable incompetence! And no leads or trails that we can follow.'

'No Janaab.'

'Alright then, in that case, we'll have to weave a web, and entrap one or two senior personnel of the High Commission.

It will not be a cakewalk. Lives will be at stake, and then the diplomatic ramifications . . . As I understand, the Indian High Commission is extremely cautious about their diplomats. They do not move in public areas and attend functions and parties collectively. So, basically, they are always on the alert and have their guard up. We have to find chinks in their armour. Do we have a source inside the High Commission?'

'Yes, Janaab.'

'Yet we didn't get any tip-off about Prem Dewan?'

'No Janaab! Our source was on leave for a month due to ill health, during the time of Prem Dewan' disappearance.'

'Oh, my goodness, even Providence favours the infidels! Anyway, let us get some tip-off about a forthcoming event. We could infiltrate that, make the strike and move out quickly.'

Colonel Iftikhar Hussain interjected, 'Janaab, we could probably get them within their premises because they are more relaxed and unguarded there. Are we looking at a complete hit? Or a cosmetic hit?'

'A complete hit, but no firearms. The finger will point directly and immediately towards the establishment; we don't want to be embarrassed. It has to look like an accident. We can't afford another diplomatic fracas of international proportions.'

'Ji Janaab. I am sure this plan will work. The High Commission is practically impenetrable. But the residences are porous: we can infiltrate without detection.'

'Moin, ask your contact to pick up the calendar of social events to be held in the near future. We will need a few days for recce and for planning a seamless entry and exit. Any other insider we are in contact with?'

'Janaab, I will connect with our sources and activate them.'

'All information, big or small, gathered from the High Commission is to be reported to me only; we have to expedite our action. The top brass is extremely agitated over this dismal failure. The Indians would be gloating over this pyrrhic victory,' lamented Sheikh.

'Colonel Iftikhar and Colonel Abdullah will coordinate with me on the action plan. Moin will provide all relevant information and ground support. I will enrol the men to make the hit. Are there any questions? If no, the operation begins as of now,' he concluded. As the three officers stood to leave, Sheikh reminded them: 'This matter is not to be discussed outside of these four walls. Is that clear?'

'Ji Janaab.' All three saluted him. The meeting was over. The mission had begun.

Striding back to his office, Moin thanked Allah that he had gotten away with a mild rebuke from the General. It could have been much worse, perhaps curtains on his military career. He now had another chance to prove his worth. This time, failure was not an option.

Moin sent for Taufeeq. The peon tapped Taufeeq on the shoulder and gave him a note with *Major Moinuddin* scribbled on it. Taufeeq tidied his uniform, smoothened his tousled hair, and readied himself to face Major Saab. He knocked at Moin's door, and entered after he heard 'Come in.'

'Good afternoon Janaab!'

'Good afternoon Taufeeq. Please sit down.'

Taufeeq sat down gingerly.

'We had a meeting with General Akram. Brigadier Aslam, Colonel Iftikhar and Colonel Abdullah Kareem were in attendance. The report prepared by you is dismal and pathetic. Everyone, including myself, is very disappointed. We are staring down the barrel of a smoking gun. It is nothing but sacrilege that such a vital person, who would hold bundles of intelligence on various aspects of Indian defence and internal security slipped through our hands undetected. We know that the entire High Commission is involved in getting Dewan out of Pakistan. Now we have to narrow it down to who exactly was involved in the getaway.'

'We don't have any information, or evidence on the involvement of any particular individual, except that fleeting input from the watchman at Hindustan Court that one military Saab was the last person seen with the Dewan family. That is all we have, so we have to move ahead on some assumptions and conjecture, and hope we make some headway. It's been almost four months now. The Indians must be having a good laugh at the incompetence of our agencies. Soon we would be ridiculed by the international community, as word gets around. Nothing remains hidden in the intelligence circles.'

Taufeeq sat across the table with downcast eyes and kept wondering, 'Is this one more occasion for a dressing down?'

Moin continued. 'Moving forward, we have a few operatives inside the Indian High Commission and some households. You will have to contact them and collect information on a daily basis. Do not share any information with them, as some may double-cross us and leave us running around in circles. Double-check the credibility of the source by actioning on the inputs you receive. Once you are convinced of the accuracy and authenticity of the information, we can put a plan in place. Report to me daily, first thing every morning, so that we have adequate reaction time.'

Though Taufeeq had bitten the dust; he was quick to learn his lesson. He sat upright in his chair and strained his ears to capture every word that Moin spoke so that he did not lose an iota of the instructions given to him.

'Do you have any questions?' asked Moin.

'No Janaab. Will activate the sleeper cells immediately.'

'And yes, do remember, we need to target a big gun to create enough ripples in the political circles of India.'

'Yes Janaab, I understand. Only the top five or six of the High Commission,' said Taufeeq and stood up to take leave.

For Timur, the daily pastime, since Taufeeq had relieved him, was to come to the office and enjoy a cup of tea in the morning, interspersed with a drag on the cigarette every now and then. He would wander around and engage in some mindless chatter with his cronies. He generally felt relaxed in life, as the weather was benign and conducive for comfortable living. Even sitting in the sun and soaking up some vitamin D was most enjoyable. He was making the most of his good time, as Taufeeq had been inordinately quiet and had not assigned any task to him. The driver too was enjoying the temporary hiatus. But this state of bliss would soon go through a tectonic shift and turn into a conundrum of frenetic activity of unpleasant and inhuman brutality.

'Saab is calling you!' an office peon whispered in Timur's ear. Timur, lazing in the sun, sprawled out with his legs resting on another chair, looked up at him with dozy eyes.

'Who is calling?'

'Taufeeq Saab.'

'Ok, Ok! I'm coming.'

Timur got up and strolled to Taufeeq's table in unhurried steps. He saw Taufeeq buried in some files and thought to himself 'Oh no! Not again!' Taufeeq looked up at Timur, 'Where have you been? I haven't seen you around in weeks.'

'Janaab was looking very tense and disturbed, so I didn't want to trouble you. But all these days I was sitting outside. If you had called me, I would have presented myself.'

'Ok, ok! That's fine.'

Taufeeq indicated to a chair and told Timur to sit down. He normally didn't do that, so Timur was a bit surprised. Nevertheless, he sat down.

'How many sources do we have in the Indian High Commission?'

'We had around four to five people Janaab. But they are not active. Some may not be there anymore. Last I was in touch with them was when we were collecting information about Dewan.'

'Yes, I understand. It is about Dewan only! Today your task will be to activate these sources and collect information about the movements of the top officials of the High Commission, what they are doing, where are they going, and if there are any upcoming events. The sources must not know who you are and must not be able to recognise you and contact you. Change your appearance as much as possible, grow your hair like a mane, shave off the moustache and wear dark glasses.'

'Contact your sources daily, change the meeting locations and timings as frequently as possible. I'll give you a slip—collect some cash from Major Moinuddin's office. Tip your sources well, lest they lose interest and withhold important information. If they ask for more, just give it. No arguments. Even you and the driver! Your food, cigarettes and tea are on the house, but I need actionable information. Report to me daily at the end of the day.'

Timur nodded and got to his feet.

'And Timur! No more loitering around on the job.'

Timur walked away, smiling. The first thing on his mind was to collect cash from Major Moin's office. Food and smoke on the house; life was good.

By the time he had pocketed the cash and made his way to the garages, it was close to 4.00 p.m. 'Too late for lunch,' he lamented, but made up for it with tea and samosas.

He summoned the driver and they drove out of the Headquarters.

Next, Timur made his way to the barbershop to shave off his moustache. He changed his hair style and the colour of his hair He also bought himself a pair of trendy sunglasses. Yippee! His disguise was in place. Their first stop for the day was the Indian High Commission. They stopped the vehicle some distance away. Timur got out of the jeep and walked towards the security cabin. He went through the motions of completing the entry in the register, made eye contact with his source and moved away into the visa office.

He took the visa application form and started filling it as the source walked by him casually. Timur placed a slip of paper under his chair so that the informer could see it. He got up slowly, dropped the application form into the trash can and left.

Once Timur had exited the building, the informer moved to the chair where he had been sitting. He picked up the slip of paper, slipped it into his pocket and went to the toilet. Timur had written 'Imtiaz bakery, 1530.' He crushed the note, put it back in his pocket and left the toilet.

Timur's next stop was Shivaji Court, where Tulsi, the butler, was his source in the Deputy High Commissioner's house. The Deputy High Commissioner's house was sanitised frequently, and housekeeping staff was recruited from India only.

In Hindustan Court, one of the housemaids, Margaret, was his source. He touched base with her too, letting her know their time and place of first contact. As decided, they all met Timur daily, but for a while, no significant information came forth. Finally, Tulsi mentioned that the Deputy High Commissioner was planning to host a dinner at his residence in a fortnight's time. Timur passed this information to Taufeeq, who in turn informed Moin, who called up Brigadier Sheikh and let him know.

Sheikh couldn't have asked for a more opportune moment than this to strike at will. He summoned a meeting in his office the same day. 'I am glad at the input I received from you Moin,' he said. 'I think this is the ideal occasion and location for us to strike. Is safe access into the bungalow assured?'

Moin replied, 'We have an Indian national on our payrolls. He has no love lost for his boss or the country due to a long-standing grudge from the Partition days. The Deputy High Commissioner is a bachelor, so there are no wives and children to worry about. I will do a recce myself, and just to make sure, a second one on the day of the strike.'

Sheikh turned to Colonel Iftikhar Hussain, 'Is your team ready?'

'Ji Janaab! I've shortlisted five young men, well trained in combat. They should measure up well to the task, more so because no weapons are being used.'

'What about the logistics, Abdullah?'

'Janaab, everything required by Iftikhar's team will be provided, including a backup in case something goes wrong. We can move in and create a diversion and make a safe exit.'

'You all know that they have diplomatic immunity. Officially we cannot enter their premises,' the Brigadier reminded them.

'Ji Janaab. We'll create the diversion outside the premises to make sure we are on safe ground.'

'Alright but be extremely cautious. Don't break any rules regarding our code of conduct and the UN Convention on Diplomats.'

'Sir, my men are bold and smart. If cornered, they may not stick to the rules of engagement,' said Iftikhar.

'I understand, Iftikhar. But I want the mission accomplished; we are not making a movie thriller. Ensure least collateral damage,' ordered the Brigadier.

'I'll brief General Akram Saab on the plan. Once I get his approval, we can go ahead and execute it.'

The plan in place, approval obtained, they now waited for the dinner to be hosted at the Deputy High Commissioner's residence on 26 January 1966.

15

The Road to Recovery

You can chain me, you can torture me, you can even destroy this body, but you will never imprison my mind.

—*MK Gandhi*[*]

Jack, drained by seething pain, was in deep sleep. Inside his mind ran a reel of images—the smiling faces of his children, his loving wife, the burble of the sea, the scent of wood and smoke. The nurse gently nudged him awake for the doctor's visit, unwittingly interrupting his blissful slumber. Pain ripped through him as he opened his eyes.

The doctor's prognosis continued to be circumspect, bordering on pessimism. Jack's pelvic bone and the head of the

---

[*] Mahatma Gandhi: Inspiring Thoughts.

femur were broken. It was doubtful whether both the bones would mend sufficiently to carry the weight of the entire body. But it was early days yet. The picture would be clearer in another four weeks.

Jack became more alert with every passing day, sleeping much less. The skin regained its lustre, his appetite improved and he started mumbling a few incoherent words. Dorothy's constant presence, her love and support strengthened his resolve to fight. He knew she believed in him. He had never been indisposed even for a day in his entire working life.

The minor fractures mended and gentle movement was not so painful anymore. The lungs had healed sufficiently, so the oxygen levels in his blood steadied, and the doctors took him off the respirator. But the femur and the hip bone, essential for him to walk again, would take another two weeks before the doctors could make the next assessment.

The children had not seen their father for nearly two months. Dorothy would say, 'Daddy is getting better. He will come home soon.'

'But you say that every day.' Debora would persist.

'Yes, but that is the truth. He will be with us soon.'

'Can you take us to meet Daddy?'

'The hospital does not allow children to come inside.'

'Please Mum, we want to see Daddy.' Debora pleaded, nudging her younger brother to say something.

So, he chipped in, 'Mum, please take us to the hospital. We want to see Daddy'.

Dorothy sat on the edge of the bed and hugged them close. Her tears melted their tender hearts, and soon they were crying too. It was hard for the children, and she understood their need to see their father. She promised them she would request the doctors to allow them a visit. Cheered up, they stopped crying and ran off to play.

A few days later, Dorothy asked the Nanny to get both the children ready to go to the hospital. Excited the children dressed quickly and ran to the car.

As Dorothy drove along, she patted her son, 'You have to be a good boy, no running around and making a noise. The hospital is for people who are not well. So, we have to not disturb them, so that they can get better soon.'

Both of them answered in one voice. 'Ok, Mum.'

On reaching the hospital, Dorothy walked holding the children by their hands, to the nursing station. 'I'm Mrs Jack Shea. My husband is in room no 612.' She told the receptionist. 'I've got special permission from the doctors for the children to meet their father. Please inform the nurses to bring my husband down to meet them.'

'Ok, I'll just check. You can wait in the waiting room.'

After about twenty minutes of impatient waiting, the nurse wheeled Jack in a wheelchair. Dorothy rose from her seat, held the children's hands and moved towards Jack. The children couldn't recognise him at first. His eyes were sunken, and he had an unkempt beard. He was leaning to one side of the wheelchair. They were shocked and a little frightened. Where was their dashing father?

As if on cue, he spoke.

'Debba! Jonfy!' His arm stretched towards them. The next instant they ran to him, flung their arms around his neck and started weeping. 'Daddy, Daddy, what happened? What happened Daddy?' They echoed. Jack held them tightly and kissed them repeatedly.

'I'm alright now. I'm coming home soon.'

They remained in a huddle for a long while, chattering excitedly.

'Don't go away again Daddy, I miss you so much,' said Debora, sniffling.

'I will never go away again, I promise,' said Jack.

After half an hour, the nurse came to take Jack back to his room.

As they were preparing to leave, Amar Singh walked into the waiting room and chatted with Dorothy for a while. She requested him to take the children home, so she could spend the night with her husband. Though a bit reluctant to leave their mother and father in the hospital, they held Amar Singh's hand and trotted off with him. They kept looking over their shoulders and waving to their parents time and time again.

Another fortnight rolled by before the doctors confirmed that the major bones in Jack's pelvic girdle and the femur had healed. Yet he needed support to rise and stand. It was obvious that he would have to undergo rigorous physiotherapy before he could attempt to walk again. Over the days, Jack made rapid progress and was soon able to take a few steps.

Three more weeks of twice-a-day physiotherapy enabled Jack to walk a fair distance with the support of a walking stick. But he had a noticeable limp that would last a lifetime and serve as a stark reminder of the brutality he had survived.

The hospital, though clean, lacked the personal touch. Jack was yearning to get back home, to be with the children, eat home-cooked food and sleep in his own bed. The doctors, pleased with Jack's progress, discharged him after two months to convalesce at home. However, he would have to visit the hospital daily for physiotherapy, and every week, his progress would be reviewed.

Jack returned home to a roaring welcome. Dorothy was overjoyed. At long last, her fervent prayers had come to fruition. The children were bouncing around like rabbits, running from house to house, sharing their joy with friends. The staff were relieved and happy that the master of the house had come home.

Jack walked to the bedroom and gazed down at the baby, who was sleeping peacefully. He picked up his little boy and cuddled him. It was difficult for him to stand for long, so he sat down, holding the baby in his arms. Happiness returned to the Shea family after an agonising gap of three months.

Dorothy needed to work on her health, too. The daily grind of rising early, attending to two young children and an infant, sitting for hours on end outside the ICU had drained her physically and emotionally. The joys of life and womanhood that Jack had lavished over her for the last fifteen years had crumbled in one fell swoop.

But now, with Jack back at home by her side, she had all the time to take care of herself. The despair was quickly replaced by joy, and she began to recoup her lost strength. At times, when the memory of the nightmare they had endured resurfaced, Jack comforted her by comparing her resolve to the lighthouse that stands tall, weathering every storm. The children would be amused to hear their father tell their mother about the lighthouse. Little Jon was too intrigued to let it pass, so he asked his father, 'What's a lighthouse, Daddy?'

'Your mother, my son, is the lighthouse of our lives,' he explained. 'One that bears the savage intensity of the waves, day and night, and yet stands steadfast giving light, strength, guidance, direction, and hope to the weary, keeping them out of harm's way.'

Slowly, Jack was able to take short walks with his walking stick. He was advised to take extreme care against lifting any weights or tripping, because a fall could be disastrous.

Jack's presence at home had a magical effect on the family. It was like Christmas time for Debora and Jon. The moment they returned from school, they would cling to him and stay with him all through the day, so much so that at night while the baby slept in his cot at the foot of his parents' bed, these two would snuggle up on either side of him, hug him tightly and listen to stories till they dozed off. The children's presence helped Jack rebuild his strength and self-confidence.

At every weekly check-up, the doctors would be pleasantly surprised at the spirit and vitality he displayed. Dorothy chuckled inwardly because she knew something that the doctors didn't— the doughty Rajput courage that her man had inherited at birth set him apart.

Soon, Jack started walking without any signs of pain, though in measured steps and with the support of a walking stick. His eyesight had normalised, he could breathe well and there was no congestion in the chest. The only limb that healed awkwardly and took time was the right arm, still in a sling. In fact, he would never be able to write again with his right hand. Jack was very conscious of this abnormality, so he would mask it cleverly.

Regular physiotherapy that grew strenuous with every passing day helped Jack regain his full physical capacity. Soon, the doctors cleared him to attend office and resume normal work.

Initially, Jack accompanied Amar in his car as he would take time to get his hand back on the wheel. Amar too was pleased to have a companion. The first day at the office, after a gap of four months, was a celebration—every member of the High Commission came to greet him with gifts and flowers. He was their hero, the soldier who had served his country and defied death.

Amar, who had thoroughly examined the site of the gory crime, was still trying to understand how the perpetrators had managed to attack Jack. One day, as they drove home from work, he turned to Jack and hesitantly asked, 'What really happened that night?'

He had barely finished his query when he noticed Jack's face turn pale, his jaw tighten. Feeling guilty, Amar murmured, 'I'm sorry, Jack. Maybe it was insensitive of me to bring it up.'

Jack clenched his fist. Then he took a deep breath and began to speak.

'You may recall I was talking with the U.S. Defence Attaché and enjoying my drink. After I took a few sips from my second drink, I started feeling nauseous. My head was spinning, as if I was having an attack of vertigo. Now I know that my drink had been spiked. I rushed into the house to use the toilet. The bearer, Tulsi, told me that some guest was already in the toilet on the ground floor. So, he helped me to the one on the first floor. The lights were off in the toilet, as I turned to switch on the lights and lock the door, somebody hit me hard on the head and I fell to the floor. It was dark so I couldn't see who it was and how many people were there, as the blows kept coming from every direction. They were hitting me with batons. I tried to fight back but two of them held me down and the others kept assaulting me. I don't know how long they clobbered me, but I remember being in extreme agony and barely conscious. They perhaps assumed that they had killed me as I could hear a faint whisper, 'mar gaya kafir' (the infidel is dead) and carried me to the terrace and threw me over the terrace walls. I passed out the moment I hit the ground.'

Amar was stunned into silence. He couldn't stomach what Jack had just recounted. He shuddered to think that instead of Jack, it could have been him. For the rest of the drive, neither of the men spoke. One was horrified at what he had heard, and the other tormented by the memories of his ordeal.

After the incident, the High Commissioner offered Jack the choice to return to India and recuperate in peace. But Jack declined, as he firmly believed in what General Patton said many years ago, 'Success is how high you bounce when you hit bottom.' The words made him more determined than ever to remodel catastrophes into opportunities. As he regained normal health, he would spend long hours at work, take on tasks beyond his remit and complete them with a flourish.

Jack spent one more year in Karachi along with his family till the end of his tenure in May 1967. Mercifully, the year went by without anything untoward in the office or at home.

For a Defence Officer, assignment in an Indian High Commission as a Defence Attaché is a defining moment in his career, as it not only gives an opportunity to work and live abroad with the family, it also is an indicator of one's upward mobility in the merit-based promotional rungs. The Sheas, an affable and charming family, cherished everything that came their way and acquitted themselves with grace in public and at home.

The physical and emotional scars they had suffered as a family taught them to face challenges with courage. They returned home much stronger and went on to achieve innumerable successes in their lives.

The family moved back to Bombay, India, at the end of May 1967. On 1 June 1967, Captain Jack Shea took over as the Commanding Officer (Captain 'D') of the 11th Destroyer Squadron, comprising INS Rajput, INS Rana and INS Ranjit, a glowing tribute to his outstanding professionalism and leadership. He commanded the fleet for a year and a half and was then posted to New Delhi to attend the National Defence College, another feather in the cap of his distinguished career.

16

The Investiture

Every individual attains fulfilment of life and fame only on account of discharging the duties prescribed for him/her.

—*The Bhagavad Gita, 18–45**

16 April 1969. The Durbar Hall of the Rashtrapati Bhavan was awash in majestic splendour, all set for the Defence Investiture Ceremony. The opulence of the hall, dazzling in the stained-glass detailing and crystal chandeliers, created a spectacular ambience befitting the occasion.

This ceremony is a once-a-year glittering event, where the President of India presents the Gallantry Awards and Distinguished Service Medals to defence personnel. Conducted

---

* Anonymous.

with all the conventions of military discipline, it is a sterling occasion in the calendar of events at Rashtrapati Bhavan.

The function was presided over by the President, Mr VV Giri, and attended by the Prime Minister, Smt Indira Gandhi, her Cabinet colleagues, selected members of the Opposition and important Government functionaries, including the Chiefs of the three Services.

Jack entered the Durbar Hall with Dorothy, resplendent in her beautiful pink silk saree with two strings of pearls. Their elder son Roger walked beside them, handsome in a three-piece black suit with shining Tuffees to match. It was a proud day for the family—he would be receiving the Ati Vishisht Sewa Medal today.

The awardees sat separately in a pre-arranged sequence. The guests took the middle rows adjacent to the seating for the Prime Minister and other dignitaries, facing the President's chair. The Master of Ceremonies (MC) lectern was to one side, visible to all. A red carpet led from the centre of the Durbar Hall up to the stage where the President was seated.

As the ceremony got underway, the recipients followed the well-rehearsed drill to rise from their chair, walk up in turn and take position at the front end of the red carpet, about 15 feet away from the President, till the MC announced their award and name. They would then march up to the President, halt two paces away from him, salute and wait for the President to pin the medal. Once done, they shook hands with the President, gave a salute and marched back to their seat.

Jack rose and took position at the designated point, facing the President.

'Ati Vishisht Seva Medal, Captain Garnet Milton Shea, Indian Navy,' announced the MC. Jack marched smartly to the President, saluted and took his position.

Tears welled up in Dorothy's eyes as her man, who she had almost lost to the brutality of the enemy, received the honour from the President of India, in the presence of the country's highest dignitaries.

As the President picked up the medal to pin it on Jack's chest, there came a loud cheer 'Yay Dad!' momentarily shattering the solemnity of the well-orchestrated function. It was Roger, of course. Dorothy, alarmed and embarrassed, tugged at his hand repeatedly to make him sit down, but to no avail.

Jack stood ramrod straight. The President, also unflinching, pinned the medal on him. Then he said, with a smile, 'Congratulations, Captain Shea! Your son is really proud of you and so is the nation.'

All dignitaries in the hall, including the Prime Minister, turned around and saw a young boy, all of eighteen years old, standing up and cheering for his father. The Prime Minister was gracious in her response; she smiled and started to applaud the young boy. What better cue than this for others to start clapping. The applause, in its crescendo, echoed in the high-ceilinged dome of the Durbar Hall, and would resound in Jack's heart for years to come, as a pleasant reminder of the audacity of his young progeny, who in a single moment of pride and excitement had celebrated his father without restraint.

After the Investiture, the guests gathered in the annexe to the Durbar Hall for high tea. It was a proud moment for the families to join the President and the Prime Minister for a cup of tea. Jack, Dorothy and Roger were invited to sit with the President, who put his hand on Roger's shoulder and said, 'You are a brave boy.' Roger was delighted. Jack and Dorothy beamed with pride.

It was truly a life-defining moment for them.

Jack also greeted the Prime Minister, the Defence Minister and a host of other dignitaries. He spotted a familiar figure— Prem Dewan, positioned now in the Prime Minister's office for Madam's personal security. He had been elevated to the top job after his return from Pakistan.

He walked towards them and clasped Jack's hand. They hugged. For a while, Prem could not speak. Then the dam of emotions broke. 'How can I ever convey my gratitude to you? You saved me from certain death and my family from the torturous clutches of those brutes. We could have been languishing in hell, without recourse to any justice or Nirmala. You put your life on the line to save us. I am aware of the brutal vengeance they wreaked on you, and all I can say is that my family and I will be indebted to you forever. Do give me an opportunity, I will always be at your service.'

Jack smiled. His eyes said it all. Given a chance, he would do it again. This was the highest call of duty; to put your life on the line and walk away with nothing but gratitude for being able to serve your nation and your fellowmen.

A quintessential 'Fauji'.

Jai Hind!

Acknowledgements

This book is an outcome of years of research, interaction and delving into the inner recesses of my mind. I owe a sincere debt of gratitude to everyone who supported me in this endeavour.

First of all, to my family, my husband Ravi, my children Amanda, Ashish, Tanya, my brothers Roger, Ian, Jon and Chris who were patient, helpful and encouraged me at every step to complete this book in time.

To my dear friends Teji Singh, Marianne de Nazareth, and Keerti Ramachandran who supported me in this initiative and gave their time to listen to the rough cuts.

To Shubhra Krishan who edited the manuscript and gave it the final shape, and who readily and graciously gave her time and inputs and suggested valuable improvements.

To Preeta Priyamvada, who provided support in the edit of the manuscript, for her guidance and structural consultancy.

Acknowledgements

My appreciation and gratitude to Sathya Saran for her unstinted support and commitment. Her conceptual ideas helped me in formatting the script correctly while keeping the focus in place.

I would like to thank Manmohan Anchan for the creatives and for designing the book cover.

I am grateful to Air Marshal SP Singh, mentor, philosopher, guide and friend, for his invaluable advice and for being a constant source of inspiration. He spent countless hours in research and editing. His vast knowledge of military and geopolitical matters helped me tremendously in writing the book.

All in all, my lifelong passion to let the world know of the immense sacrifices of my father, Jack Shea, way beyond the call of duty, wouldn't have come to fruition without the blessings of the Almighty.

—